D0108653

MINGO

by

joel chandler harris

LITERATURE HOUSE / GREGG PRESS
Upper Saddle River, N. J.

Republished in 1970 by
LITERATURE HOUSE
an imprint of The Gregg Press
121 Pleasant Avenue
Upper Saddle River, N. J. 07458

Standard Book Number–8398-0764-3
Library of Congress Card–76-104477

JOEL CHANDLER HARRIS

Joel Chandler Harris was born in 1848 near Eatonton, Putnam County, Georgia. His mother came from an upper-class Southern family, and his father was a feckless, charming Irish laborer who disappeared shortly before the birth of the child. A well-to-do neighbor, Mr. Andrew Reid, took the mother and her boy under his protection, and Joel was sent to a local academy for his education. He was an indifferent student, however, and preferred the joys of rural life to books. As a result, his schooling terminated at the age of thirteen, when, in response to a want ad, he took a job as printer's devil with the *Countryman*, a popular weekly newspaper published on the plantation of Joseph A. Turner. Harris found a second protector in Mr. Turner, who gave him the use of his library. When Turner discovered that his protégé was anonymously placing articles in the *Countryman*, he did everything possible to encourage him to write. It was while living on the Turner plantation that Joel absorbed the Negro legends and folklore, as well as the slave dialect, which appeared years later in the Uncle Remus tales. At the age of sixteen he wrote his first attempt at Cracker speech— a letter to Lincoln admonishing the President to leave the Capital faster "than a sheep can skin a 'simmon tree," signed "Obediah Skinflint." Later in life Harris became an admirer of Lincoln.

Harris saw many of his friends go off to the War, and in 1865, when the carnage had ended, he found himself the possessor of some worthless Confederate currency and no job. He went to Macon, Georgia, and by luck was hired to work in the composing room of the *Macon Telegraph*. He then made his way to New Orleans, where the Editor of the *Crescent Monthly* hired him as a private secretary. He became acquainted with Lafcadio Hearn, but that bizarre, cosmopolitan writer and the boisterous, backwoods Georgia lad had little in common. Harris apparently did not feel at home in New Orleans, and in 1867 returned to Eatonton to "nurse a novel." The novel did not materialize; instead he took yet another newspaper job, this time with the *Monroe Advertiser*, which he left three years later in order to accept the associate editorship of the Savannah *Morning News*. While in Savannah he met Esther La Rose, whom he married, and who presented him with nine children.

In 1876, Harris, his wife, and "two bow legged children" appeared in Atlanta, where the *Atlanta Constitution* hired him to write a column containing a humorous Negro character. This was Harris' last newspaper job, and the beginning of the Uncle Remus series, the greatest works in the literature of American Negro folklore.

The publication of *Uncle Remus, His Songs and His Sayings* in 1880 made Harris famous. This is a collection of thirty-four stories told by an aged Negro to a young white boy. They have been translated into practically every European language as well as into African dialects, and there are at least five different editions presently in print. They were the basis for one of Walt Disney's most delightful films. *Nights With Uncle Remus*, a second series of tales, appeared in 1883. Here, the narrator is *Coast Negro Daddy Jack*, who speaks the Gullah dialect, which is drawn from numerous African languages and is not at all easy to follow. Harris published several more collections of Uncle Remus stories, the best of which are *Uncle Remus and His Friends* (1892), *Told by Uncle Remus* (1905), and *Uncle Remus and the Little Boy* (1910).

Although Harris is best known for the Uncle Remus books, he also wrote two novels, a series of children's stories, and three novelettes. *Sister Jane* (1896) is an idyllic novel of Georgia life before the War. *Gabriel Tolliver: A Story of Reconstruction* (1902) is an excellent, dispassionate study of the effects of military government upon the South. In *Mingo and Other Sketches in Black and White* (1884), Harris examines the class lines which divide the middle class from the aristocrats, and exclude the Negroes from intercourse with either. *Free Joe and Other Georgia Sketches* (1887) deals with master-slave relationships. The title story is a pathetic tale of an emancipated slave who can find no place in society. *On the Wing of Occasions* (1900) contains humorous non-dialect stories, the best of which is "The Kidnapping of President Lincoln." The theme of these stories is reconciliation.

Harris held his position with the *Atlanta Constitution* for twenty-four years. In 1900 he signed a contract with the McClure Phillips Company. Seven years later he founded *Uncle Remus' Magazine*. Don Marquis was associate editor, and had his own by-line, and Ludwig Lewisohn wrote articles for it. After *Uncle Remus' Magazine* merged with the *Home Magazine*, Harris continued to write Uncle Remus stories. Theodore Roosevelt, one of the rare American presidents to take an interest in letters, was fond of Harris' stories, and after Harris' death in 1902 helped to keep *Uncle Remus' Magazine* going.

Upper Saddle River, N. J.   F. C. S.
December, 1969

MINGO

AND OTHER

SKETCHES IN BLACK AND WHITE

BY

JOEL CHANDLER HARRIS

AUTHOR OF "NIGHTS WITH UNCLE REMUS," "UNCLE REMUS: HIS
SONGS AND HIS SAYINGS," ETC.

BOSTON
JAMES R. OSGOOD AND COMPANY
1884

University Press:
JOHN WILSON AND SON, CAMBRIDGE.

CONTENTS.

———◆———

MINGO:

A SKETCH OF LIFE IN MIDDLE GEORGIA.

MINGO:

A SKETCH OF LIFE IN MIDDLE GEORGIA.

I.

IN 1876, circumstances, partly accidental and partly sentimental, led me to revisit Crooked Creek Church, near the little village of Rockville, in Middle Georgia. I was amazed at the changes which a few brief years had wrought. The ancient oaks ranged roundabout remained the same, but upon everything else time had laid its hand right heavily. Even the building seemed to have shrunk; the pulpit was less massive and imposing, the darkness beyond the rafters less mysterious. The preacher had grown gray, and feebleness had taken the place of that physical vigor which was formerly the distinguishing feature of his interpretations of the larger problems of theology. People I had never seen sat in the places of those I had known so well. There were only traces here and there of the old congregation, whose austere simplicity had made so deep an impression upon my youthful mind. The blooming girls of 1860 had grown into careworn matrons, and the young men had developed in their features the strenuous uncertainty and misery of the period of desolation and disaster through which they had passed. Anxiety had so ground itself into their lives that a stranger to the manner might well have been pardoned for giving a sinister interpretation to these pitiable manifestations of hopelessness and unsuccess.

I had known the venerable preacher intimately in the past; but his eyes, wandering vaguely over the congregation, and resting curiously upon me, betrayed no recognition. Age, which had whitened his hair and enfeebled his voice, seemed also to have given him the privilege of ignoring everything but the grave and the mysteries beyond.

These swift processes of change and decay were calculated to make a profound impression, but my attention was called away from all such reflections. Upon a bench near the pulpit, in the section reserved for the colored members, sat an old negro man whose face was perfectly familiar. I had known him in my boyhood as Mingo, the carriage-driver and body-servant of Judge Junius Wornum. He had changed but little. His head was whiter than when I saw him last; but his attitude was as firm and as erect, and the evidences of his wonderful physical strength as apparent, as ever. He sat with his right hand to his chin, his strong serious face turned contemplatively toward the rafters. When his eye chanced to meet mine, a smile of recognition lit up his features, his head and body drooped forward, and his hand fell away from his face, completing a salutation at once graceful, picturesque, and imposing.

I have said that few evidences of change
manifested themselves in Mingo; and so it
seemed at first, but a closer inspection showed
one remarkable change. I had known him
when his chief purpose in life seemed to be to
enjoy himself. He was a slave, to be sure, but
his condition was no restraint upon his spirits.
He was known far and wide as " Laughing
Mingo," and upon hundreds of occasions he
was the boon companion of the young men
about Rockville in their wild escapades. Many
who read this will remember the " 'possum
suppers" which it was Mingo's delight to pre-
pare for these young men, and he counted
among his friends and patrons many who afterward became distinguished both in war and
in the civil professions. At these gatherings
Mingo, bustling around and serving his guests,
would keep the table in a roar with his quaint
sayings and local satires in the shape of im-
promptu doggerel; and he would also repeat
snatches of orations which he had heard in
Washington when Judge Wornum was a mem-

ber of Congress. But his chief accomplishments lay in the wonderful ease and fluency with which he imitated the eloquent appeals of certain ambitious members of the Rockville bar, and in his travesties of the bombastic flights of the stump-speakers of that day.

It appeared, however, as he sat in the church, gazing thoughtfully and earnestly at the preacher, that the old-time spirit of fun and humor had been utterly washed out of his face. There was no sign of grief, no mark of distress, but he had the air of settled anxiety belonging to those who are tortured by an overpowering responsibility. Apparently here was an interesting study. If the responsibilities of life are problems to those who have been trained to solve them, how much more formidable must they be to this poor negro but lately lifted to his feet! Thus my reflections took note of the pathetic associations and suggestions clustering around this dignified representative of an unfortunate race.

Upon this particular occasion church services

were to extend into the afternoon, and there was an interval of rest after the morning sermon, covering the hour of noon. This interval was devoted by both old and young to the discussion of matters seriously practical. The members of the congregation had brought their dinner baskets, and the contents thereof were spread around under the trees in true pastoral style. Those who came unprovided were, in pursuance of an immemorial custom of the section and the occasion, taken in charge by the simple and hearty hospitality of the members.

Somehow I was interested in watching Mingo. As he passed from the church with the congregation, and moved slowly along under the trees, he presented quite a contrast to the other negroes who were present. These, with the results of their rural surroundings superadded to the natural shyness of their race, hung upon the outskirts of the assembly, as though their presence was merely casual, while Mingo passed along from group to group of his white friends and acquaintances with that familiar and confident air of meritorious humility and unpretentious dignity which is associated with good-breeding and gentility the world over. When he lifted his hat in salutation, there was no servility in the gesture; when he bent his head, and dropped his eyes upon the ground, his dignity was strengthened and fortified rather than compromised. Both his manners and his dress retained the flavor of a social system the exceptional features of which were too often, by both friend and foe, made to stand for the system itself. His tall beaver, with its curled brim, and his blue broadcloth dress-coat, faded and frayed, with its brass buttons, bore unmistakable evidence of their age and origin; but they seemed to be a reasonable and necessary contribution to his individuality.

Passing slowly through the crowd, Mingo made his way to a double-seated buggy shielded from all contingencies of sun and rain by an immense umbrella. From beneath the seat he drew forth a large hamper, and proceeded to arrange its contents upon a wide bench which stood near.

While this was going on, I observed a tall, angular woman, accompanied by a bright-looking little girl, making her way toward Mingo's buggy. The woman was plainly, even shabbily, dressed, so that the gay ribbons and flowers worn by the child were gaudy by contrast. The woman pressed forward with decision, her movements betraying a total absence of that undulatory grace characteristic of the gentler sex, while the little girl dancing about her showed not only the grace and beauty of youth, but a certain refinement of pose and gesture calculated to attract attention.

Mingo made way for these with ready deference, and after a little I saw him coming toward me. He came forward, shook hands, and remarked that he had brought me an invitation to dine with Mrs. Feratia Bivins.

"Miss F'raishy 'members you, boss," he said, bowing and smiling, "en she up 'n' say she be mighty glad er yo' comp'ny ef you kin put up wid cole vittles an' po' far'; en ef you come," he added on his own account, "we like it mighty well."

II.

ACCEPTING the invitation, I presently found myself dining with Mrs. Bivins, and listening to her remarkable flow of small talk, while Mingo hovered around, the embodiment of active hospitality.

"Mingo 'lowed he'd ast you up," said Mrs. Bivins, " an' I says, says I, 'Don't you be a-pesterin' the gentulmun, when you know thar's plenty er the new-issue quality ready an' a-waitin' to pull an' haul at 'im,' says I. Not that I begrudges the vittles, — not by no means ; I hope I hain't got to that yit. But somehow er 'nother folks what hain't got no great shakes to brag 'bout gener'ly feels sorter skittish when strange folks draps in on 'em. Goodness knows, I hain't come to that pass wher' I begrudges the vittles that folks eats, bekaze anybody betweenst this an'

Clinton, Jones County, Georgy, 'll tell you the Sanderses wa'n't the set to stint the'r stomachs. I was a Sanders 'fore I married, an' when I come 'way frum pa's house hit was thes like turnin' my back on a barbecue. Not by no means was I begrudgin' of the vittles. Says I, 'Mingo,' says I, 'ef the gentulmun is a teetotal stranger, an' nobody else hain't got the common perliteness to ast 'im, shorely you mus' ast 'im,' says I; 'but don't go an' make no great to-do,' says I, 'bekaze the little we got mightent be satisfactual to the gentulmun,' says I. What we got may be little enough, an' it may be too much, but hit's welcome."

It would be impossible to convey an idea of the emphasis which Mrs. Bivins imposed upon her conversation. She talked rapidly, and yet with a certain deliberation of manner which gave a quaint interest to everything she said. She had thin gray hair, a prominent nose, firm thin lips, and eyes that gave a keen and sparkling individuality to sharp and homely features. She had evidently seen sorrow and defied it. There was no suggestion of compromise in manner or expression. Even her hospitality was uncompromising. I endeavored to murmur my thanks to Mrs. Bivins for Mingo's thoughtfulness, but her persistent conversation drowned out such poor phrases as I could hastily frame.

"Come 'ere, Pud Hon," continued Mrs. Bivins, calling the child, and trimming the demonstrative terms of "Pudding" and "Honey" to suit all exigencies of affection, — "come 'ere, Pud Hon, an' tell the gentulmun howdy. Gracious me! don't be so *countrified.* He ain't a-gwine to *bite* you. No, sir, you won't fine no begrudgers mixed up with the *Sanderses.* Hit useter be a *common* sayin' in Jones, an' cle'r 'cross into Jasper, that pa would 'a' bin a rich man an' 'a' owned *niggers* if it had n't but 'a' bin bekase he sot his head ag'in stintin' of his stomach. That's what they useter say, — use n't they, Mingo?"

"Dat w'at I year tell, Miss F'raishy — sho'," Mingo assented, with great heartiness. But Mrs. Bivins's volubility would hardly wait for this perfunctory indorsement. She talked as she arranged the dishes, and occasionally she would hold a piece of crockery suspended in the air as she emphasized her words. She dropped into a mortuary strain: —

"Poor pa! I don't never have nothin' extry an' I don't never see a dish er fried chicken but what pa pops in my mind. A better man hain't never draw'd the breath of life, — that they hain't. An' he was thes as gayly as a kitten. When we gals'd have comp'ny to dinner, pore pa he'd cut his eye at me, an' up an' say, says he, 'Gals, this 'ere turkey's mighty nice, yit I'm reely afeared you put too much inguns in the dressin'. Maybe the young men don't like 'em as good as you all does;' an' then pore pa'd drap his knife an' fork, an' laugh tell the tears come in his eyes. Sister Prue she useter run off an' have a cry, but I let you know I was one er the kind what wa'n't so easy sot back.

"I'd 'a' bin mighty glad if Pud yer had er took airter pa's famerly, but frum the tip eend er her toe nails to the toppermust ha'r of her head she's a Wornum. Hit ain't on'y thes a

streak yer an' a stripe thar, — hit's the whole
bolt. I reckon maybe you know'd ole Jedge
June Wornum; well, Jedge June he was Pud's
gran'pa, an' Deely Wornum was her ma.
Maybe you might 'a' seed Deely when she was
a school-gal."

Cordelia Wornum! No doubt my astonishment made itself apparent, for Mrs. Bivins
bridled up promptly, and there was a clearly
perceptible note of defiance in her tone as she
proceeded.

"Yes, sir-ree! *An' make no mistake!* Deely
Wornum married my son, an' Henry Clay
Bivins made 'er a good husbun', if I do have
to give it out myse'f. Yes, 'ndeed! An' yit
if you'd 'a' heern the rippit them Wornums
kicked up, you'd 'a' thought the pore chile'd
done took 'n' run off 'long of a whole passel er
high pirates frum somewheres er 'nother. In
about that time the ole Jedge he got sorter
fibbled up, some say in his feet, an' some say in
his head; but his wife, that Em'ly Wornum,
she taken on awful. I never seen her a-gwine

on myse'f; not that they was any hidin' out
'mongst the Bivinses er the Sanderses, — bless
you, no! bekaze here's what wa' n't afeared er
all the Wornums in the continental State er
Georgy, not if they'd 'a' mustered out under
the lead er ole Nick hisse'f, which I have my
doubts if he wa' n't somewheres aroun'. I
never seen 'er, but I heern tell er how she was
a-cuttin' up. You may n't think it, but that
'oman taken it on herse'f to call up all the
niggers on the place an' give 'em her forbid-
dance to go an' see the'r young mistiss."

" Yit I lay dey tuck 'n' sneak 'roun' en come
anyhow, ain't dey, Miss F'raishy?" inquired
Mingo, rubbing his hands together and smiling
blandly.

" *That* they did, — *that* they did! " was Mrs.
Bivins's emphatic response. " Niggers is niggers, but them Wornum niggers was a cut er
two 'bove the common run. I 'll say that, an'
I 'll say it on the witness stan'. Freedom
might 'a' turned the'r heads when it come to
t' other folks, but hit did n't never turn the'r

heads 'bout the'r young mistiss. An' if Mingo
here hain't done his juty 'cordin' to his lights,
then I dunner what juty is. I 'll say that open
an' above-board, high an' low."

The curious air of condescension which Mrs.
Bivins assumed as she said this, the tone of
apology which she employed in paying this
tribute to Mingo and the Wornum negroes,
formed a remarkable study. Evidently she
desired me distinctly to understand that in
applauding these worthy colored people she was
in no wise compromising her own dignity.

Thus Mrs. Bivins rattled away, pausing only
long enough now and then to deplore my lack
of appetite. Meanwhile Mingo officiated around
the improvised board with gentle affability;
and the little girl, bearing strong traces of her
lineage in her features, — a resemblance which
was confirmed by a pretty little petulance of
temper, — made it convenient now and again
to convey a number of tea cakes into Mingo's
hat, which happened to be sitting near, the
conveyance taking place in spite of laughable

paritomimic protests on the part of the old man
ranging from appealing nods and grimaces to
indignant gestures and frowns.

"When Deely died," Mrs. Bivins went on,
waving a towel over a tempting jar of preserves,
"they wa' n't nobody but what was afeared to
break it to Emily Wornum, an' the pore chile 'd
done been buried too long to talk about before
her ma heern tell of it, an' then she drapped
like a clap er thunder had hit 'er.   Airter so
long a time, Mingo thar he taken it 'pun hisse'f
to tell 'er, an' she flopped right down in 'er
tracks, an' Mingo he hepped 'er into the house,
an', bless your life, when he come to he'p 'er
out 'n it, she was a changed 'oman.   'T wa' n't
long 'fore she taken a notion to come to my
house, an' one mornin' when I was a-washin'
up dishes, I heern some un holler at the gate,
an' thar sot Mingo peerched up on the Wornum
carry-all, an' of all livin' flesh, who should be
in thar but ole Emily Wornum!

"Hit 's a sin to say it," continued Mrs. Bivins,
smiling a dubious little smile that was not with-

out its serious suggestions, "but I tightened up
my apern strings, an' flung my glance aroun'
tell hit drapped on the battlin'-stick, bekaze I
flared up the minnit I seen 'er, an' I says to
myse'f, says I, ' If hit's a fracas you er huntin',
my lady, I lay you won't hafter put on your
specs to fine it.' An' then I says to Pud,
says I, —

" ' Pud Hon, go in the shed-room thar, chile,
an' if you hear anybody a-hollerin' an' a-squallin'
ther', shet your eyeleds an' grit your teeth,
bekaze hit'll be your pore ole granny a-tryin'
to git even with some er your kin.'

" An' then I taken a cheer an' sot down by
the winder. D'reckly in come Emily Wornum,
an' I wish I may die if I'd 'a' know'd 'er if
I'd saw 'er anywheres else on the face er the
yeth. She had this 'ere kinder dazzled look
what wimmen has airter they bin baptized in
the water. I helt my head high, but I kep'
my eye on the battlin'-stick, an' if she'd 'a'
made fight, I'd be boun' they'd 'a' bin some
ole sco'es settled then an' thar if ole sco'es

ken be settled by a frailin'. But, bless your
heart, they wa'n't never no cammer 'oman than
what Emily Wornum was; an' if you'd 'a'
know'd 'er, an' Mingo wa'n't here to b'ar me
out, I wish I may die if I would n't be afeared
to tell you how ca'm an' supjued that 'oman
was, which in her young days she was a tarri-
fier. She up an' says, says she,—

"'Is Mizzers Bivins in?'

"'Yessum,' says I, 'she is that-away. An'
more'n that, nobody don't hafter come on this
hill an' holler more'n twicet 'thout gittin'
some kinder answer back. *Yessum!* An'
what's more, Mizzers Bivins is come to that
time er life when she's mighty proud to git
calls from the big-bugs. If I had as much
perliteness, ma'am, as I is cheers, I'd ast
you to set down,' says I.

"She stood thar, she did, thes as cool as a
cowcumber; but d'reckly she ups an' says,
says she,—

"'Might I see my little gran'chile?' says
she.

"' Oho, ma'am!' says I; 'things is come to a mighty purty pass when quality folks has to go frum house to house a-huntin' up pore white trash, an' a-astin' airter the'r kin. Tooby shore! tooby shore! Yessum, a mighty purty pass,' says I."

I cannot hope to give even a faint intimation of the remarkable dramatic fervor and earnestness of this recital, nor shall I attempt to describe the rude eloquence of attitude and expression; but they seemed to represent the real or fancied wrongs of a class, and to spring from the pent-up rage of a century.

" I wa' n't lookin' fer no compermise, nuther," Mrs. Bivins continued. " I fully spected 'er to flar' up an' fly at me; but 'stedder that, she kep' a-stan'in' thar lookin' thes like folks does when they er runnin' over sump'n in the'r min'. Then her eye lit on some er the pictur's what Deely had hung up on the side er the house, an' in pertic'lar one what some er the Wornum niggers had fetched 'er, whar a great big dog was a-watchin' by a little bit er baby.

When she seen that, bless your soul, she thes sunk right down on the floor, an' clincht 'er han's, an' brung a gasp what looked like it might er bin the last, an' d'reckly she ast, in a whisper, says she, —

" ' Was this my dear daughter's room ? '

" Maybe you think," said Mrs. Bivins, regarding me coldly and critically, and pressing her thin lips more firmly together, if that could be, — " maybe you think I oughter wrung my han's, an' pitied that 'oman kneelin' thar in that room whar all my trouble was born an' bred. Some folks would 'a' flopped down by 'er, an' I won't deny but what hit come over me; but the nex' minnit hit flashed acrost me as quick an' hot as powder how she 'd 'a' bin a-houndin' airter me an' my son, an' a-treatin' us like as we 'd 'a' bin the offscourin's er creation, an' how she cast off her own daughter, which Deely was as good a gal as ever draw'd the breath er life, — when all this come over me, hit seem like to me that I could n't keep my paws off 'n 'er. I hope the Lord 'll forgive

me, — that I do, — but if hit had n't but 'a' bin
for my raisin', I 'd 'a' jumped at Emily Wornum
an' 'a' spit in 'er face an' 'a' clawed 'er eyes
out 'n 'er. An' yit, with ole Nick a-tuggin' at
me, I was a Christun 'nuff to thank the Lord
that they was a tender place in that pore
mizerbul creetur's soul-case.

"When I seen her a-kneelin' thar, with 'er
year-rings a-danglin' an' 'er fine feathers a-
tossin' an' a-trimblin', leetle more an' my
thoughts would 'a' sot me afire. I riz an' I
stood over her, an' I says, says I, —

"'Emily Wornum, whar you er huntin' the
dead you oughter hunted the livin'. What's
betwix' you an' your Maker *I* can't tell,' says
I, 'but if you git down on your face an' lick
the dirt what Deely Bivins walked on, still
you won't be humble enough for to go whar
she's gone, nor good enough nuther. She
died right yer while you was a-traipsin' an'
a-trollopin' roun' frum pos' to pillar a-upholdin'
your quality idees. These arms helt 'er,'
says I, 'an' ef hit had n't but 'a' bin for *her*,

Emily Wornum,' says I, 'I 'd 'a' strangled the
life out 'n you time your shadder darkened my
door. An' what's more,' says I, 'ef you er
come to bother airter Pud, *thes make the trial
of it. Thes so much as lay the weight er your
little finger on 'er,*' says I, '*an I'll grab you
by the goozle an' t'ar your haslet out,*' says I."

Oh, mystery of humanity! It was merely
Mrs. Feratia Bivins who had been speaking,
but the voice was the voice of Tragedy. Its
eyes shone; its fangs glistened and gleamed;
its hands clutched the air; its tone was husky
with suppressed fury; its rage would have
stormed the barriers of the grave. In another
moment Mrs. Bivins was brushing the crumbs
from her lap, and exchanging salutations with
her neighbors and acquaintances; and a little
later, leading her grandchild by the hand, she
was making her way back to the church, where
the congregation had begun to gather.

III.

For my own part, I preferred to remain under the trees, and I soon found that this was the preference of Mingo. The old man had finished his dinner, and sat at the foot of a gigantic oak, gazing dreamily at the fleecy clouds that sailed across the sky. His hands were clasped above his head, and his attitude was one of reflection. The hymn with which the afternoon services were opened came through the woods with a distinctness that was not without a remote and curious suggestion of pathos. As it died away, Mingo raised himself slightly, and said, in a tone that was intended to be explanatory, if not apologetic, —

"Miss F'raishy, ef she ain't one sight, den I ain't never seed none. I s'pec' it seem sorter funny ter you, boss, but dat w'ite 'oman done had lots er trouble; she done had bun-

nunce er trouble — she sholy is! Look mighty
cu'us dat some folks can't git useter yuther
folks w'at got Ferginny ways, but dat's Miss
F'raishy up en down. Dat's her, sho'! Ole
Miss en ole Marster dey had Ferginny ways,
en Miss F'raishy she would n't 'a' stayed in a
ten-acre fiel' wid um, — dat she would n't.
Folks w'at got Ferginny ways, Miss F'raishy
she call um big-bugs, en she git hos*tile* w'en
she year der name call. Hit's de same way
wid niggers. Miss F'raishy she hate de common run er niggers like dey wuz pizen. Yit
I ain't makin' no complaints, kaze she mighty
good ter me. I goes en I suns myse'f in Miss
F'raishy back peazzer all day Sundays, w'en
dey ain't no meetin's gwine on, en all endurin'
er de week I hangs 'roun' en ploughs a little
yer, en hoes a little dar, en scratches a little
yander, en looks arter ole Miss' gran'chile.
But des let 'n'er nigger so much ez stick der
chin cross de yard palin's, en, bless yo' soul,
you'll year Miss F'raishy blaze out like de
woods done cotch afire."

Mingo paused here to chuckle over the discomfiture and alarm of the imaginary negro who had had the temerity to stick his supposititious chin over the fence. Then he went on : —

"I dunner whar Miss F'raishy git de notion 'bout dat chile a-faverin' er de Wornums, kaze she de ve'y spit en image er ole Miss, en ole Miss wuz a full-blood Bushrod. De Bushrods is de fambly what I cum fum myse'f, kaze w'en ole Miss marry Marster, my mammy fell ter her, en w'en I got big 'nuff, dey tuck me in de house fer ter wait on de table en do er'n's, en dar I bin twel freedom come out. She 'uz mighty high-strung, ole Miss wuz, yit I sees folks dese days put on mo' a'rs dan w'at ole Miss ever is. I ain't 'sputin' but w'at she hilt 'er head high, en I year my mammy say dat all the Bushrods in Ferginny done zactly dat a way.

"High-strung yer, headstrong yander," continued Mingo, closing one eye, and gazing at the sun with a confidential air. "Ef it had n't er bin fer de high-strungity-head-strongityness er de Bushrod blood, Miss Deely would n't 'a' never runn'd off wid Clay Bivins in de roun' worril, dough he 'uz des one er de nicest w'ite mens w'at you 'mos' ever laid yo' eyes on. Soon ez she done dat, wud went 'roun' fum de big house dat de nigger w'at call Miss Deely name on dat plantation would be clap on de cote-house block, en ole Miss she shot 'erse'f up, she did, en arter dat mighty few folks got a glimpse un 'er, 'ceppin' hit 'uz some er de kin, en bless yo' soul, *dey* hatter look mighty prim w'en dey come whar she wuz. Ole Marster he ain't say nothin', but he tuck a fresh grip on de jimmy-john, en it got so dat, go whar you would, dey wa' n't no mo' lonesomer place on de face er de yeth dan dat Wornum plantation, en hit look like ruination done sot in. En den, on top er dat, yer come de war, en Clay Bivins he went off en got kilt, en den freedom come out, en des 'bout dat time Miss Deely she tuck 'n' die.

"I 'clar' ter gracious," exclaimed Mingo, closing his eyes and frowning heavily, "we'n I looks back over my shoulder at dem times, hit seem like it mighty funny dat any un us pull thoo.

Some did en some did n't, en dem w'at did, dey
look like deyer mighty fergitful. W'en de smash
come, ole Marster he call us niggers up, he did,
en 'low dat we 'uz all free. Some er de boys
'low dat dey wuz a-gwineter see ef dey wuz free
sho 'nuff, en wid dat dey put out fer town, en
some say ef dey wuz free dey wuz free ter stay.
Some talk one way en some talk 'n'er. I let
you know I kep' my mouf shot, yit my min' 'uz
brim-ful er trouble.

"Bimeby soon one mornin' I make a break.
I wrop up my little han'ful er duds in a
hankcher, en I tie de hankcher on my walkin'-
cane, en I put out arter de army. I walk en I
walk, en 'bout nine dat night I come ter Ingram
Ferry. De flat wuz on t'er side er de river,
en de man w'at run it look like he gone off
some'r's. I holler en I whoop, en I whoop en
I holler, but ef dey wuz any man 'roun', he
wuz hidin' out fum me. Arter so long I got
tired er whoopin' en hollerin', en I went ter
de nighest house en borrer'd a chunk, en built
me a fier by de side er de road, en I set dar

en nod twel I git sleepy, en den I pull my
blanket 'cross my head en quile up — en when
I do dat, it's good-by, Mingo!

"Boss," said Mingo, after a little pause,
"you don't b'leeve in no ghos'es en ha'nts en
sperrits, does you?"

An apparently irrelevant inquiry, suddenly
put, is sometimes confusing, and I fear I did
not succeed in convincing Mingo of my un-
belief.

"Some does en some don't," he continued,
"but ez fer me, you kin des put me sorter
'twix' en 'tween. Dey mout be ghos'es en
den ag'in dey moutent. Ole nigger like me
ain't got no bizness takin' sides, en dat w'at
make I say w'at I does. I ain't mo'n kivver
my head wid dat blanket en shot my eyes, 'fo'
I year somebody a-callin' un me. Fus' hit
soun' way off yander.

"'*Mingo! — O Mingo!*' en den hit got
nigher — '*Mingo! — O Mingo!*'

"I ain't 'spon' ter dat, but I lay dar, I did,
en I say ter myse'f, —

" ' Bless gracious ! de man on t'er side done come ; but how in de name er goodness is he know Mingo ? '

" I lay dar, en I study en I lissen, en I lissen en I study ; en den I doze off like, en fus' news I know yer come de call, —

" ' *Mingo ! — O Mingo !* '

" Hit soun' nigher, yit hit seem like it come fum a mighty fur ways, en den wiles I wundin' en studyin', yer she come mo' plainer dan befo', —

" ' O Mingo ! '

" I snatch de blanket off 'n my head, en sot up en lissen, I did, en den I make answer, —

" ' Who dat callin' Mingo 'way out yer ? '

" I lissen en I lissen, but nobody ain't callin'. I year de water sneakin' 'long under de bank, en I year de win' squeezin' en shufflin' 'long thoo de trees, en I year de squinch-owl shiver'n' like he cole, but I ain' year no callin'. Dis make me feel sorter jubous like, but I lay down en wrop up my head.

" I ain't bin dar long 'fo' bimeby yer come

de call, en it soun' right at me. Hit rise en
it fall, en de wud wuz, —

"' *Mingo! — O Mingo!   Whar   my   little
baby?   My little baby, Mingo!   Whar my little baby?*'

"En den, boss, hit seem like I year sump'n
like a 'oman cryin' in de dark like 'er heart
gwineter break. You kin laff ef you mineter,
but I ain't dast ter take dat blanket off'n my
head, kaze I know my young mistiss done
come back, en mo'n dat, I know she uz stannin'
dar right over me.

"Tooby sho', I wuz skeer'd; but I wa'n't so
skeer'd dat I dunner w'at she mean, en I des
broke inter de bigges' kinder boo-hoo, en I
say, sez I, —

"' Make yo' peace, Miss Deely! make yo'
peace, honey! kaze I gwine right back ter dat
baby ef de Lord spar' me. I gwine back, Miss
Deely! I gwine back!'

"Bless yo' soul, boss, right den en dar I
know'd w'at bin a-pester'n' un me, kaze des
time I make up my min' fer ter come back ter

dat baby, hit look like I see my way mo' cle'r
dan w at it bin befo'. Arter dat I lay dar, I
did, en I lissen en I lissen, but I ain't year no
mo' callin' en no mo' cryin'; en bimeby I tuck
de blanket fum off 'n my head, en lo en beholes,
de stars done fade out, en day done come, en
dey wa' n't no fuss nowhars. De squinch-owl
done hush, en de win' done gone, en it look
like de water done stop sneakin' en crawlin'
und' de bank.

"I riz up, I did, en shuck de stiffness out 'n
my bones, en I look 'way 'cross de river ter
de top er de hill whar de road lead. I look
en I say, sez I, —

"'Maybe you leads ter freedom, but, bless
God! I gwine back.'

"Des 'bout dat time I see de fe'ymun come
down ter de flat en onloose de chain, en make
ez he wuz comin' 'cross arter me. Wid dat
I raise up my hat en tip 'im a bow, en dat's
de las' I seed un 'im.

"I come back, I did," continued Mingo,
reflectively, "en yer I is, en yer I bin; en I

ain't come none too soon, en I ain't stay
none too close, n'er, kaze I dunner w'at mout
er happin. Miss F'raishy been mighty good,
too, sho'. She ain't useter niggers like some
w'ite folks, en she can't git 'long wid um, but
she puts up wid me mighty well. I tuck holt
er de little piece er groun' w'at she had, en
by de he'p er de Lord we bin gittin' on better
dan lots er folks. It bin nip en tuck, but ole
tuck come out ahead, en it done got so now dat
Miss F'raishy kin put by some er de cotton
money fer ter give de little gal a chance w'en
she git bigger. 'T won't b'ar tellin' how smart
dat chile is. She got Miss Deely peanner, en,
little ez she is, she kin pick mos' all de chunes
w'at 'er mammy useter pick. She sets at de
peanner by de hour, en whar she larnt it I be
bless ef *I* kin tell you, — dat I can't!"

The little girl had grown tired of the services
in the church, and ran out just as the old man
had put my horse to the buggy. Mingo knew
a shorter road to Rockville than that by which
I had come, and, taking the child by the hand,

he walked on ahead to show me the way. In a little while we came to the brow of a hill, and here I bade the old man and his charge good-by, and the two stood watching me as I drove away. Presently a cloud of dust rose between us, and I saw them no more; but I brought away a very pretty picture in my mind, — Mingo with his hat raised in farewell, the sunshine falling gently upon his gray hairs, and the little girl clinging to his hand and daintily throwing kisses after me.

AT TEAGUE POTEET'S.

A SKETCH OF THE HOG MOUNTAIN RANGE.

AT TEAGUE POTEET'S.

A SKETCH OF THE HOG MOUNTAIN RANGE.

I.

EMIGRATION is a much more serious matter than revolution. Virtually, it is obliteration. Thus, Gérard Petit, landing upon the coast of South Carolina in the days of French confusion, — a period covering too many dates for a romancer to be at all choice in the matter, — gave his wife and children over to the oblivion of a fatal fever. Turning his face westward, he pushed his way to the mountains. He had begun his journey fired with the despair of an exile, and he ended it with something of the energy and enterprise of a pioneer. In the foot-hills of the mountains he came to the small stream of English colonists that was then trick-

ling slowly southward through the wonderful valleys that stretch from Pennsylvania to Georgia,
between the foot-hills of the Blue Ridge and
the great Cumberland Range.   Here, perhaps
for the first time, the *je, vous, nous* of France
met in conflict the "ah-yi," the "we uns" and
the "you uns" of the English-Pennsylvania-
Georgians.   The conflict was brief.   There was
but one Gérard Petit, and, although he might
multiply the *je, vous, nous* by the thousands and
hundreds of thousands, as he undoubtedly did,
yet, in the very nature of things, the perpetual
volley of "you uns" and "we uns" must carry
the day.   They belonged to the time, and the
climate suited them.   By degrees they fitted
themselves to Gérard Petit; they carried him
from the mountains of South Carolina to the
mountains of North Georgia, and there they
helped him to build a mill and found a family.
But their hospitality did not end there.   With
the new mill and the new family, they gave him
a new name.   Gérard Petit, presumably with
his hand upon his heart, as became his race,

made one last low bow to genealogy. In his place stood Jerd Poteet, "you uns" to the left of him, "we uns" to the right of him. He made such protest as he might. He brought his patriotism to bear upon the emergency, and named his eldest son Huguenin Petit. How long this contest between hospitality on the one hand and family pride and patriotism on the other was kept up, it is unnecessary to inquire. It is enough to say that the Huguenin of one generation left Hugue Poteet as his son and heir; Hugue left Hague, and this Hague, or a succeeding one, by some mysterious development of fate, left Teague Poteet.

Meanwhile the restless stream of English-Pennsylvania-Georgians, with its "you uns" and its "we uns," trickled over into Alabama, where some of the Petits who were carried with it became Pettys and Pettises. The Georgia settlements, however, had been reinforced by Virginians, South Carolinians, and Georgians. The gold excitement brought some; while others, set adrift by the exigencies of the plantation system,

found it easier and cheaper to get to North
Georgia than to reach Louisiana or Mississippi.
Thus, in 1859, Teague Poteet, a young man of
thirty or thereabouts, was tilling, in a half-
serious, half-jocular way, a small farm on Hog
Mountain, in full view of Gullettsville. That is
to say, Poteet could see the whole of Gullettsville, but Gullettsville could not, by any means,
see the whole, nor even the half, of Poteet's
fifty-acre farm. Gullettsville could see what
appeared to be a gray notch on the side of the
mountain, from which a thin stream of blue
smoke flowed upward and melted into the blue
of the sky, and this was about all that could be
seen. Gullettsville had the advantage in this,
that it was the county-seat. A country road,
straggling in from the woods, straggled around
a barnlike structure called the court-house, and
then straggled off to some other remote and
lonely settlement.

Upon rare occasions Teague made his appearance on this straggling street, and bought his
dram and paid his thrip for it; but, in a general

way, if Gullettsville wanted to see him, it had to
search elsewhere than on the straggling street.
By knocking the sheriff of the county over the
head with a chair, and putting a bullet through
a saloon-keeper who bullied everybody, Poteet
won the reputation of being a man of marked
shrewdness and common-sense, and Gullettsville
was proud of him, in a measure. But he never
liked Gullettsville. He wore a wool hat, a
homespun shirt, jeans pantaloons, and cotton
suspenders, and he never could bring himself
into thorough harmony with the young men who
wore ready-made clothes, starched shirts, and
beaver hats; nor was his ideal of feminine
beauty reached by the village belles, with their
roach-combs, their red and yellow ribbons, and
their enormous flounces. In the mountains, he
was to the manner born; in the village, he was
keenly alive to the presence and pressure of the
exclusiveness that is the basis of all society,
good, bad, or indifferent; and it stirred his
venom. His revolt was less pronounced and
less important than that of his ancestors; but

it was a revolt. Gérard Petit left France, and
Teague Poteet remained away from Gullettsville.
Otherwise there was scarcely a trace of his lin-
eage about him, and it is a question whether he
inherited this trait from France or from the
Euphrates, — from Gérard or from Adam.

But he did not become a hermit by any means.
The young men of Gullettsville made Sunday
excursions to his farm, and he was pleased to
treat them with great deference. Moreover, he
began to go upon little journeys of his own
across Sugar Valley. He made no mystery of
his intentions; but one day there was considerable astonishment when he rode into Gullettsville on horseback, with Puss Pringle behind
him, and informed the proper authorities of his
desire to make her Mrs. Puss Poteet. Miss
Pringle was not a handsome woman, but she
was a fair representative of that portion of the
race that has poisoned whole generations by
improving the frying-pan and perpetuating
"fatty bread." The impression she made upon
those who saw her for the first time was one

of lank flatness, — to convey a vivid idea rather
clumsily. But she was neither lank nor flat.
The total absence of all attempts at artificial
ornamentation gave the future Mrs. Poteet an
appearance of forlorn shiftlessness that was not
even slightly justified by the facts. She was a
woman past the heyday of youth, but of considerable energy, and possessed of keen powers
of observation. Whatever was feminine about
her was of that plaintive variety that may be
depended upon to tell the story of whole generations of narrow, toilsome, and unprofitable
lives.

There was one incident connected with Miss
Pringle's antenuptial ride that rather intensified
the contempt which the Mountain entertained
for the Valley. As she jogged down the street,
clinging confidently, if not comfortably, to
Teague Poteet's suspenders, two young ladies of
Gullettsville chanced to be passing along. They
walked slowly, their arms twined about each
other's waists. They wore white muslin dresses,
and straw hats with wide and jaunty brims, and

the loose ends of gay ribbons fluttered about them. These young ladies, fresh from school, and no doubt full of vainglory, greeted the bridal procession with a little explosion of giggles, and when Puss Pringle pushed back her gingham sun-bonnet and innocently gazed upon them, they turned up their noses, sniffed the air scornfully, and made such demonstrations as no feminine mind, however ignorant in other directions, could fail to interpret.

Miss Pringle had not learned the art of tossing her head and sniffing the air, but she half closed her eyes, and gave the young ladies a look that meant something more than scorn. She said nothing to Teague, for she was in hopes he had not observed the tantrums of the school-girls.

But Teague saw the whole affair, and he was cut to the quick. In addition to the latent pride of his class, he inherited the sensitiveness of his ancestors; but he made no demonstration. Turning his eyes neither to the right nor to the left, he jogged along to the wedding. He carried his wife home, and thereafter avoided Gullettsville. When he was compelled to buy coffee and sugar, or other necessary luxuries, he rode forty miles across the mountain to Villa Ray.

He had been married a year or more when, one afternoon, he was compelled to ride down to Gullettsville under whip and spur for a doctor. There was a good deal of confused activity in the town. Old men and young boys were stirring around with blue cockades in their hats, and the women wore blue rosettes on their bosoms. Three negroes in uniform — a contribution from the nearest railroad town — were parading up and down the straggling street with fife and drums, and a number of men were planting a flag-pole in front of the court-house.

No conscientious historian can afford to ignore a coincidence, and it so happened that upon the very day that Teague Poteet's wife presented him with the puzzle of a daughter, Fate presented his countrymen with the problem of war. That night, sitting in the door of his house and smoking his pipe, Teague witnessed

other developments of the coincidence. In the
next room the baby-girl squalled most persis-
tently; down in the Valley the premonitions of
war made themselves heard through the narrow
throat of a small cannon which, until then, had
been used only to celebrate the Fourth of July.

The noise of a horse's hoofs roused Teague's
hounds, and some one called out from the road:

"Hello, Poteet!"

"Ah-yi!"

"You hearn the racket?"

"My gal-baby keeps up sich a hollerin' I can't
hear my own years."

"*Oh!*"

"You better b'lieve! Nine hours ole, an'
mighty peart. What's them Restercrats in the
Valley cuttin' up the'r scollops fer?"

"Whoopin' up se*says*ion. Sou' Ca'liny done
plum gone out, an' Georgy a-gwine."

Teague Poteet blew a long, thin cloud of
home-made tobacco-smoke heavenward, leaned
back heavily in his chair, and replied,—

"Them air Restercrats kin go wher' they

dang please; I'm a-gwine to stay right slam-bang in the Nunited States."

There was a little pause, as if the man on horseback was considering the matter. Then the response came, —

"Here's at you!"

"Can't you 'light?" asked Poteet.

"Not now," said the other; "I'll git on furder."

The man on horseback rode on across the mountain to his home. Another mountaineer, seeing the rockets and hearing the sound of the cannon, came down to Poteet's for information. He leaned over the brush-fence.

"What's up, Teague?"

"Gal-baby; reg'lar surbinder."

"*Shoo!* won't my ole 'oman holler! What's up down yan?"

"Them dad-blasted Restercrats a-secedin' out'n the Nunited States."

"They say they er airter savin' of the'r niggers," said the man at the fence.

"Well, I hain't got none, and I hain't a-

4

wantin' none; an' it hain't been ten minnits sense I ups an' says to Dave Hightower, s' I, ' The Nunited States is big enough for me.' "

" Now you er makin' the bark fly," said the man at the fence.

During the night other men came down the mountain as far as Poteet's, and always with the same result.

The night broadened into day, and other days and nights followed. In the Valley the people had their problem of war, and on the Mountain Teague Poteet had the puzzle of his daughter. One was full of doubt and terror and death, and the other full of the pleasures of peace. As the tide of war surged nearer and nearer, and the demand for recruits became clamorous, the people of the Valley bethought them of the gaunt but sturdy men who lived on the Mountain. A conscript officer, representing the necessities of a new government, made a journey thither, — a little excursion full of authority and consequence. As he failed to return, another officer, similarly equipped and commissioned,

rode forth and disappeared, and then another
and another ; and it was not until a little search
expedition had been fitted out that the Confed-
erates discovered that the fastnesses of Hog
Mountain concealed a strong and dangerous
organization of Union men. There was a good
deal of indignation in the Valley when this state
of affairs became known, and there was some
talk of organizing a force for the purpose of
driving the mountaineers away from their homes.
But somehow the Valley never made up its
mind to attack the Mountain, and, upon such
comfortable terms as these, the Mountain was
very glad to let the Valley alone.

After awhile the Valley had larger troubles
to contend with. Gullettsville became in some
measure a strategic point, and the left wing of
one army and the right wing of the other ma-
nœuvred for possession. The left wing finally
gave way, and the right wing marched in and
camped round about, introducing to the distracted inhabitants General Tecumseh Sherman
and some of his lieutenants. The right wing

had learned that a number of Union men were concealed on the mountain, and one or two little excursion parties were made up for the purpose of forming their acquaintance. These excursions were successful to this extent, that some of the members thereof returned to the friendly shelter of the right wing with bullet-holes in them, justly feeling that they had been outraged. The truth is, the Poteets and the Pringles and the Hightowers of Hog Mountain had their own notions of what constituted Union men. They desired to stay in the United States on their own terms. If nobody pestered them, they pestered nobody.

Meanwhile Teague Poteet's baby had grown to be a thumping girl, and hardly a day passed that she did not accompany her father in his excursions. When the contending armies came in sight, Teague and his comrades spent a good deal of their time in watching them. Each force passed around an elbow of the mountain, covering a distance of nearly sixty miles, and thus for days and weeks this portentous panorama was spread out before these silent watchers. Surely never before did a little girl have two armies for her playthings. The child saw the movements of the soldiers, the glitter of the array, and the waving of the banners; she heard the dull thunder of the cannon, and the sharp rattle of the musketry. When the sun went down, and the camp-fires shone out, it seemed that ten thousand stars had fallen at her feet, and sometimes sweet strains of music stole upward on the wings of the night, and slipped heavenward through the sighing pines.

The gray columns swung right and left, and slowly fell back; the blue columns swayed right and left, and slowly pressed forward, — sometimes beneath clouds of sulphurous smoke, sometimes beneath heavy mists of rain, sometimes in the bright sunshine. They swung and swayed slowly out of sight, and Hog Mountain and Gullettsville were left at peace.

The child grew and thrived. In the midst of a gaunt and sallow generation, she shone radiantly beautiful. In some mysterious way she inherited the beauty and grace and refinement of a Frenchwoman. Merely as a phenomenon, she ought to have reminded Teague of his name and lineage; but Teague had other matters to think of. "Sis hain't no dirt-eater," he used to say; and to this extent only would he commit himself, his surroundings having developed in him that curious excess of caution and reserve which characterizes his class.

As for Puss Poteet, she sat and rocked herself and rubbed snuff, and regarded her daughter as one of the profound mysteries. She was in a state of perpetual bewilderment and surprise, equalled only by her apparent indifference. She allowed herself to be hustled around by Sis without serious protest, and submitted, as Teague did, to the new order of things as quietly as possible.

Meanwhile the people in the Valley were engaged in adjusting themselves to the changed condition of affairs. The war was over, but it had left some deep scars here and there, and those who had engaged in it gave their attention to healing these, — a troublesome and interminable task, be it said, which by no means kept pace with the impatience of the victors, whipped into fury by the subtle but ignoble art of the politician. There was no lack of despair in the Valley, but out of it all prosperity grew, and the promise of a most remarkable future. Behind the confusion of politics, of one sort and another, the spirit of Progress rose and shook her ambitious wings.

Something of all this must have made itself felt on the Mountain, for one day Teague Poteet pushed his wide-brimmed wool hat from over his eyes with an air of astonishment. Puss had just touched upon a very important matter.

" I reckon in reason," she said, " we oughter pack Sis off to school some'rs. She 'll thes nat'ally spile here."

" Hain't you larnt her how to read an' write an' cipher ? " asked Teague.

" I started in," said Mrs. Poteet, " but, Lord ! I hain't more 'n opened a book tell she know'd more 'n I dast to know ef I wuz gwine to die fer it. Hit 'll take somebody iots smarter 'n' stronger 'n me."

Teague laughed, and then relapsed into seriousness. After awhile he called Sis. The girl came running in, her dark eyes flashing, her black hair bewitchingly tangled, and her cheeks flushing with a color hitherto unknown to the Mountain.

"What now, pap?"

"I wuz thes a-thinkin' ef maybe you ought n't to bresh up an' start to school down in Gullettsville."

"Oh, pap!" the girl exclaimed, clapping her hands with delight. She was about to spring upon Teague and give him a severe hugging, when suddenly her arms dropped to her side, the flush died out of her face, and she flopped herself down upon a chair. Teague paid no attention to this.

"Yes, siree," he continued, as if pursuing a well-developed line of argument; "when a gal gits ez big ez you is, she hain't got no business to be a-gwine a-whoopin' an' a-hollerin' an' a-rantin' an' a-rompin' acrost the face er the yeth. The time's done come when they oughter be tuck up an' made a lady out 'n; an' the nighest way is to sen' 'em to school. That's whar youer a-gwine, — down to Gullettsville to school."

"I sha'n't, an' I won't, — I won't, I won't, *I won't!*" exclaimed Sis, clenching her hands and stamping her feet. "I 'll *die* first."

Teague had never seen her so excited.

"Why, what's the matter, Sis?" he asked, with unfeigned concern.

Sis gave him a withering look.

"Pap, do you reckon I 'm fool enough to traipse down to Gullettsville an' mix with them people, wearin' cloze like these? Do you reckon I 'm fool enough to make myself the laughin'-stock for them folks?"

Teague Poteet was not a learned man, but he was shrewd enough to see that the Mountain had a new problem to solve. He took down his rifle, whistled up his dogs, and tramped skyward. As he passed out through his horse-lot, the cap and worm of a whiskey-still lying in the corner of the fence attracted his attention. He paused and turned the apparatus over with his foot. It was old and somewhat battered.

"I'll thes about take you," said Teague, with a chuckle, "an' set up a calico-factory. I'll heat you up an' make you spin silk an' split it into ribbens."

It was a case of civilization or no civilization; and there is nothing more notorious in history, nothing more mysterious, than the fact that civilization is not over-nice in the choice of her handmaidens. One day it is war, another it is slavery. Every step in the advancement of the human race has a paradox of some kind as a basis. In the case of Sis Poteet, it was whiskey.

Teague got his still together, and planted it in a nice cool place, where it could be reached only by a narrow foot-path. He had set up a still immediately after the war, but it had been promptly broken up by the revenue officers. Upon this occasion, therefore, he made elaborate preparations to guard against surprise and detection, and these preparations bore considerable fruit in the way of illicit whiskey; the ultimate result of which was that Sis went to school in Gullettsville, and became the belle of the town.

It came to pass that the breath of the Mountain was heavily charged with whiskey, and the Government got a whiff of it. Word went to Washington, and there was much writing and consulting by mail, and some telegraphing. The officials — marshal, deputy marshals, and collector — were mostly men from a distance, brought hither on the tide of war, who had no personal interest in judging the situation. Naturally enough, the power with which they were invested was neither discreetly nor sympathetically exercised. They represented the Government, which they were taught to believe by the small men above them was still at war with every condition and belief in Georgia.

Down in the Valley they domineered with impunity; and one fine morning a posse, armed with carbines, rode up the Mountain, laughing, talking, and rattling their gear as gayly as a detachment of cuirassiers parading under the protection of friendly guns. The Mountain was inhospitable; for when they rode down again, a few hours afterward, three saddles were empty, and the survivors had a terrible story to tell of an attack from an unseen foe.

By the time the story of this fight with the illicit distillers reached Washington, the details were considerably magnified. The Commissioner was informed by the Marshal that a detail of deputy marshals had attempted to seize a still and were driven back by an overpowering force. The correspondents at the Capital still further enlarged the details, and the affair finally went into history as " A New Phase of the Rebellion." This was the natural outgrowth of the confusion of that period; for how should the careless deputy marshals, thinking only of the sectionalism that lit up the smouldering ruins of war, know that the Moonshiners were Union men and Republicans ?

While the Government was endeavoring to

invent some plan for the capture of the Moonshiners, Sis Poteet was growing lovelier every
day. She was a great favorite with the teachers
of the academy and with everybody. As a general thing she avoided the public square when
riding to and from the school; but it was hats
off with all the men when she did go clattering
down the street, and some of the romantic dry-
goods clerks sent their sighs after her. Sighs
are frequently very effective with school-girls,
but those that followed Sis Poteet fell short and
were wasted on the air; and she continued to
ride from the Mountain to the Valley and from
the Valley to the Mountain in profound ignorance of the daily sensation she created among
the young men of Gullettsville, to whom her
fine figure, her graceful ways, and her thrillingly
beautiful face were the various manifestations of
a wonderful revelation.

Naturally enough, the Government took no
account of Sis Poteet. The Commissioner at
Washington conferred with the Marshal for
Georgia by mail, and begged him to exert him

self to the utmost to break up the business of
illicit distilling in the Hog Mountain Range. In
view of an important election about to be held in
some doubtful State in the North or West, the
worthy Commissioner at Washington even suggested the propriety of another armed raid, to
be made up of deputy marshals and a detachment of men from the Atlanta garrison. But
the Marshal for Georgia did not fall in with this
suggestion. He was of the opinion that if a raid
was to be made at all it should not be made
blindly, and he fortified his opinion with such an
array of facts and arguments that the Bureau
finally left the whole matter to his discretion.

Early one morning, in the summer of 1879, a
stranger on horseback rode up the straggling
red road that formed the principal business
thoroughfare of Gullettsville, and made his way
toward the establishment known as the Gullettsville Hotel. The chief advertisement of the
hotel was the lack of one. A tall, worm-eaten
post stood in front of the building, but the frame
in which the sign had swung was empty. This

post, with its empty frame, was as significant as the art of blazonry could have made it. At any rate, the stranger on horseback — a young man — pressed forward without hesitation. The proprietor himself, Squire Lemuel Pleasants, was standing upon the low piazza as the young man rode up. The squire wore neither coat nor hat. His thumbs were caught behind his suspenders, giving him an air of ease or of defiance, as one might choose to interpret, and his jaws were engaged in mashing into shape the first quid of the morning.

As the young man reined up his horse at the door, Squire Pleasants stepped briskly inside and pulled a string which communicated with a bell somewhere in the back yard.

"This is the Gullettsville Hotel, is it not?" the young man asked.

"Well, sir," responded the squire, rubbing his hands together, "sence you push me so clost, I'll not deny that this here's the tavern. Some calls it the hotel, some calls it the Pleasants House, some one thing, an' some another;

but as for me, I says to all, says I, ' Boys, it 's a plain tavern.' In Fergeenia, sir, in my young days, they wa' n't nothin' better than a tavern. 'Light, sir, 'light," continued the hospitable squire, as a tow-headed stable-boy tumbled out at the door in response to the bell ; " drap right down an' come in."

The young man followed the landlord into a bare little office, where he was given to understand in plain terms that people who stopped with Squire Pleasants were expected to make themselves completely at home. With a pen upon which the ink had been dry for many a day the young man inscribed his name on a thin and dirty register, — " Philip Woodward, Clinton, Georgia ;" whereupon the squire, with unnecessary and laborious formality, assigned Mr. Woodward to a room.

Judging from appearance, the United States Marshal for Georgia had not gone astray in selecting Woodward to carry out the delicate mission of arranging for a successful raid upon Hog Mountain. Lacking any distinguishing

trait of refinement or culture, his composure
suggested the possession of that necessary information which is the result of contact with
the world and its inhabitants. He had that
large air of ease and tranquillity which is born
of association, and which represents one of the
prime elements of the curious quality we call
personal magnetism. He was ready-witted, and
full of the spirit of adventure. He was the
owner of the title to a land-lot somewhere in the
neighborhood of Hog Mountain, and this land-
lot was all that remained of an inheritance that
had been swept away by the war. There was a
tradition — perhaps only a rumor — among the
Woodwards that the Hog Mountain land-lot
covered a vein of gold; and to investigate this
was a part of the young man's business in
Gullettsville, entirely subordinate, however, to
his desire to earn the salary attached to his
position.

The presence of a stranger at the hospitable
tavern of Squire Pleasants attracted the attention of the old and young men of leisure, and

the most of them gathered upon the long, narrow piazza to discuss the matter. Uncle Jimmy Wright, the sage of the village, had inspected the name in the register and approved of it. He had heard of it before, and he proceeded to give a long and rambling account of whole generations of Woodwards. Jake Cohen, a pedler, who with marvellous tact had fitted himself to the conditions of life and society in the mountains, and who was supposed to have some sort of connection with the traffic in " blockade " whiskey, gave some reminiscences of a family of Woodwards in Ohio. Tip Watson, who had a large local reputation for humor, gravely inquired of Squire Pleasants if the new-comer had left any message for him.

Doubtless the squire, or some one else, would have attempted a facetious reply to Mr. Watson ; but just then a tall, gaunt, gray-haired, grizzly-bearded man stepped upon the piazza, and saluted the little gathering with an awkward wave of the hand. The not unkindly expression of his face was curiously heightened (or deepened) by the alertness of his eyes, which had the quizzical restlessness we sometimes see in the eyes of birds or animals. It was Teague Poteet, and the greetings he received were of the most .effusive character.

"Howdy, boys, howdy!" he said, in response to the chorus. "They hain't airy one er you gents kin split up a twenty-dollar chunk er greenbacks, is they?"

Tip Watson made a pretence of falling in a chair and fainting; but he immediately recovered, and said in a sepulchral whisper, —

"Ef you find anybody dead, an' they ain't got no twenty-dollar bill on their person, don't come a-knockin' at my door. Lord!" he continued, "look at Cohen's upper lip a-trimblin'. He wants to take that bill out somewheres an' hang it on a clothes-line."

"Ow!" exclaimed Cohen, "yoost lizzen at date man! Date Teep Vatsen, he so foony as allt tem utter peoples put tergetter. Vait, Teague, vait! I chanche date pill right avay, terreckerly."

But Teague was absorbed in some information which Squire Pleasants was giving him.

"He don't favor the gang," the squire was saying, with emphasis, "an' I'll be boun' he ain't much mixed up wi' 'em. He's another cut. Oh, they ain't a-foolin' me this season of the year," he continued, as Teague Poteet shook his head doubtfully; "he ain't mustered out'n my mind yit, not by a dad-blamed sight. I'm jest a-tellin' of you; he looks spry, an' he ain't no sneak, — I'll swar to that on the stan'."

"Well, I tell you, square," responded Teague, dryly, "I hain't never seed people too purty to pester yuther folks; an' I reckon you ain't nuther, is you?"

"No," said Squire Pleasants, his experience appealed to instead of his judgment; "no, I ain't, that's a fact; but some folks youer bleege to take on trus'."

Further comment on the part of Poteet and the others was arrested by the appearance of Woodward, who came out of his room, walked rapidly down the narrow hall-way and out upon the piazza. He was bareheaded, his hands were full of papers, and he had the air of a man of business. The younger men who had gathered around Squire Pleasants and Teague Poteet fell back loungingly as Woodward came forward with just the faintest perplexed smile.

"Judge Pleasants," he said, "I'm terribly mixed up, and I'll have to ask you to unmix me."

The squire cleared his throat, adjusted his spectacles, and straightened himself in his chair. The title of Judge, and the easy air of deference with which it was bestowed, gave him an entirely new idea of his own importance. He frowned judicially as he laid his hand upon the papers.

"Well, sir," said he, "I'm gittin' ole, an' I reckon I ain't much, nohow; I'm sorter like the gray colt that tried to climb in the shuck-pen,—I'm weak, but willin'. Ef you'll jest whirl in an' make indication whar'in I can he'p, I'll do the best I kin."

"I've come up here to look after a lot of land," said Woodward. "It is described here as lot No. 18, 376th district, Georgia Militia, part of land lot No. 11, in Tugaloo, formerly Towaliga County. Here is a plat of Hog Mountain, but somehow I can't locate the lot."

The squire took the papers and began to examine them with painful particularity.

"That 'ar lot," said Teague Poteet, after awhile, "is the ole Mathis lot. The line runs right across my simblin' patch, an' backs up ag'in' my hoss-stable."

"Tooby shore,— tooby shore!" exclaimed the squire. "Tut-tut! What am I doin'? My mind is drappin' loose like seed-ticks from a shumake bush. Tooby shore, it's the Mathis lot. Mr. Wooderd, Mr. Poteet — Mr. Poteet, Mr. Wooderd; lem me make you interduced, gents."

Mr. Woodward shook hands gracefully and cordially,— Poteet awkwardly and a trifle suspiciously.

"It seems to me, Mr. Poteet," said Woodward, "that I have seen your name in the papers somewhere."

"Likely," replied Poteet; "they uv bin a mighty sight er printin' gwine on sence the war, so I 've heern tell. Ef you 'd a-drapped in at Atlanty, you mought er seed my name mixt up in a warrant."

" How is that?" Woodward asked.

" Bekaze I bin a-bossin' my own affa'rs."

Poteet had straightened himself up, and he looked at Woodward with a steadiness which the other did not misunderstand. It was a look which said, " If you 've got that warrant in your pocket, it won't be safe to pull it out in these diggin's."

Squire Pleasants recognized the challenge that made itself heard in Teague Poteet's voice.

" Yes, yes," he said, in a cheerful tone, " our folks is seen some mighty quare doin's sence the war; but times is a-gittin' a long ways better now."

" Better, hell!" exclaimed Sid Parmalee.

What he would have said further, no one can know; for the voluminous voice of Cohen broke in, —

" Tlook ow-ut, t'ere, Sid! tlook ow-ut! t'at pad man kedge you!"

This remarkable admonition was received with a shout of laughter. Good humor was restored; and it was increased when Woodward, shortly afterward, drinking with the boys at Nix's saloon, called for three fingers of Mountain Dew, and washed it down with the statement that it tasted just as nice as liquor that had been stamped by the Government. In short, Woodward displayed such tact and entered with such heartiness into the spirit of the people around him that he disarmed the trained suspicions of a naturally suspicious community. Perhaps this statement should be qualified. Undoubtedly the marshal, could he have made a personal inspection of Woodward and his surroundings, would have praised his subordinate's tact. The truth is, while he had disarmed their suspicions, he had failed utterly to gain their confidence.

With a general as well as a particular interest in the direction of Hog Mountain, it was natural that Deputy Marshal Woodward should meet or overtake Miss Poteet as she rode back and forth between Gullettsville and the gray notch in the mountain known as Poteet's. It was natural, too, that he should take advantage of the social informalities of the section and make her acquaintance. It was an acquaintance in which Woodward and, presumably, the young lady herself became very much interested; so that the spectacle of this attractive couple galloping along together over the red road that connected the Valley with the Mountain came to be a familiar one. And its effect upon those who paused to take note of it was not greatly different from the effect of such spectacles in other sections. Some looked wise and shook their heads sorrowfully; some smiled and looked kindly, and sent all manner of good wishes after the young people. But whether they galloped down the Mountain in the fresh hours of the morning, or ambled up its dark slope in the dusk of the evening, neither Woodward nor Sis Poteet gave a thought to the predictions of spite or to the prophecies of friendliness.

The Mountain girl was a surprise to Wood-

ward.   She had improved her few opportunities
to the utmost.   Such information as the Gullettsville Academy afforded she relished and absorbed, so that her education was thorough as
far as it went.   Neither her conversation nor
her manners would have attracted special attention in a company of fairly bright young girls,
but she formed a refreshing contrast to the
social destitution of the Mountain region.

Beyond this, her personality was certainly
more attractive than that of most women, being
based upon an independence which knew absolutely nothing of the thousand and one vexatious
little aspirations that are essential to what is
called social success.   Unlike the typical American girl, whose sweetly severe portraits smile
serenely at us from the canvas of contemporary
fiction, Miss Poteet would have been far from
equal to the task of meeting all the requirements
of perfectly organized society; but she could
scarcely have been placed in a position in which
her natural brightness and vivacity would not
have attracted attention.

At any rate, the indefinable charm of her presence, her piquancy, and her beauty was a perpetual challenge to the admiration of Deputy Marshal Woodward. It pursued him in his dreams, and made him uncomfortable in his waking hours; so much so, indeed, that his duties as a revenue officer, perplexing at best, became a burden to him.

In point of fact, this lively young lady was the unforeseen quantity in the problem which Woodward had been employed to solve; and, between his relations to the Government and his interest in Sis Poteet, he found himself involved in an awkward predicament. Perhaps the main features of this predicament, baldly presented, would have been more puzzling to the authorities at Washington than they were to Woodward; but it is fair to the young man to say that he did not mistake the fact that the Moonshiner had a daughter for an argument in favor of illicit distilling, albeit the temptation to do so gave him considerable anxiety.

In the midst of his perplexity, Deputy Marshal Woodward concluded that it would be better for the Government, and better for his own peace of mind, if he allowed Sis Poteet to ride home without an escort; and for several days he left her severely alone, while he attended to his duties, as became a young fellow of fair business habits.

But one afternoon, as he sat on the piazza of the hotel nursing his confusion and discontent, Sis Poteet rode by. It was a tantalizing vision, though a fleeting one. It seemed to be merely the flash of a red feather, the wave of a white hand, to which Woodward lifted his hat; but these were sufficient. The red feather nodded gayly to him, the white hand invited. His horse stood near, and in a few moments he was galloping toward the Mountain with the Moonshiner's daughter.

When the night fell at Teague Poteet's on this particular evening, it found a fiddle going. The boys and girls of the Mountain, to the number of a dozen or more, had gathered for

a frolic, — a frolic that shook the foundations
of Poteet's castle, and aroused echoes familiar
enough to the good souls who are fond of the
cotillon in its primitive shape. The old folks
who had accompanied the youngsters sat in
the kitchen with Teague and his wife; and here
Woodward also sat, listening with interest to
the gossip of what seemed to be a remote era, —
the war and the period preceding it.

The activity of Sis Poteet found ample scope,
and, whether lingering for a moment at her
father's side like a bird poised in flight, or moving lightly through the figures of the cotillon,
she never appeared to better advantage.

Toward midnight, when the frolic was at its
height, an unexpected visitor announced himself.
It was Uncle Jake Norris, who lived on the far
side of the Mountain. The fiddler waved his
bow at Uncle Jake, and the boys and girls cried,
" Howdy," as the visitor stood beaming and
smiling in the doorway. To these demonstrations Uncle Jake, " a chunk of a white man
with a whole heart," as he described himself,

made cordial response, and passed on into the kitchen. The good humor of Mr. Norris was as prominent as his rotundity. When he was not laughing, he was ready to laugh. He seated himself, looked around at the company, and smiled.

"It's a long pull betwixt this an' Atlanty," he said after awhile; "it is that, certain an' shore, an' I hain't smelt of the jug sence I lef' thar. Pull 'er out, Teague, — pull 'er out."

The jug was forthcoming.

"Now, then," continued Uncle Jake, removing the corn-cob stopper, "this looks like home, sweet home, ez I may say. It does, certain an' shore. None to jine me? Well, well! Times change an' change, but the jug is company for one. So be it. Ez St. Paul says, cleave nigh unto that which is good. I'm foreswore not to feel lonesome tell I go to the gallows. Friends! you uv got my good wishes, one an' all!"

"What's a-gwine on?" asked Poteet.

"The same," responded Uncle Jake, after swallowing his dram. "Allers the same. Wick-

edness pervails well-nigh unto hits own jestifi-
cation. I uv seed sights! You all know the
divers besettings whar'by Jackson Ricks wuz
took off this season gone, — murdered, I may
say, in the teeth of the law an' good govunment.
Sirs! I sot by an' seed his besetters go scotch-
free."

"Ah!"

The exclamation came from Teague Poteet.

"Yes, sirs! yes, friends!" continued Uncle
Jake, closing his eyes and tilting his chair back.
"Even so. Nuther does I boast ez becometh the
fibble-minded. They hurried an' skurried me
forth an' hence, to mount upon the witness-stan'
an' relate the deed. No deniance did I make.
Ez St. Paul says, sin, takin' occasion by the
commandment, worked in me all manner of con-
spicuessence. I told 'em what these here eyes
had seed.

"They errayed me before jedge an' jury,"
Uncle Jake went on, patting the jug affection-
ately, "an' I bowed my howdies. 'Gentermun
friends,' s' I, 'foller me clost, bekaze I'm a-givin'

you but the truth, stupendous though it be.
Ef you thes but name the word,' s' I, 'I 'll take
an' lay my han' upon the men that done this
unrighteousness, for they stan' no furder than
yon' piller,' s' I. 'Them men,' s' I, ' surroundered
the house of Jackson Ricks, gentermun friends,
he bein' a member of Friendship Church, an'
called 'im forth wi' the ashoreance of Satan an'
the intents of evil,' s' I; 'an' ole en decrippled
ez he wuz, they shot 'im down, — them men
at yon' piller,' s' I, ' ere he could but raise his
trimblin' han' in supplication; an' the boldest
of 'em dast not to face me here an' say nay,'
s' I."

"An' they uv cler'd the men what kilt pore
Jackson Ricks!" said Teague, rubbing his grizzled chin.

"Ez clean an' ez cle'r ez the pa'm er my
han'," replied Uncle Jake, with emphasis.

The fiddle in the next room screamed forth
a jig, and the tireless feet of the dancers kept
time, but there was profound silence among
those in the kitchen. Uncle Jake took advan-

tage of this pause to renew his acquaintance with the jug.

Deputy Marshal Woodward knew of the killing of Jackson Ricks; that is to say, he was familiar with the version of the affair which had been depended upon to relieve the revenue officers of the responsibility of downright murder; but he was convinced that the story hinted at by Uncle Jake Norris was nearer the truth.

As the young man rode down the Mountain, leaving the fiddle and the dancers to carry the frolic into the gray dawn, he pictured to himself the results of the raid that he would be expected to lead against Hog Mountain, — the rush upon Poteet's, the shooting of the old Moonshiner, and the spectacle of the daughter wringing her hands and weeping wildly. He rode down the Mountain, and before the sun rose he had written and mailed his resignation. In a private note to the marshal, enclosed with this document, he briefly but clearly set forth the fact that, while illicit distilling was as unlawful as ever, the man who

6

loved a Moonshiner's daughter was not a proper instrument to aid in its suppression.

But his letter failed to have the effect he desired, and in a few weeks he received a communication from Atlanta setting forth the fact that a raid had been determined upon.

Meantime, while events were developing, some of the old women of the Hog Mountain Range had begun to manifest a sort of motherly interest in the affairs of Woodward and Sis Poteet. These women, living miles apart on the Mountain and its spurs, had a habit of "picking up their work" and spending the day with each other. Upon one occasion it chanced that Mrs. Sue Parmalee and Mrs. Puritha Hightower rode ten miles to visit Mrs. Puss Poteet.

"Don't lay the blame of it onter me, Puss," exclaimed Mrs. Hightower, — her shrill, thin voice in queer contrast with her fat and jovial appearance; "don't you lay the blame onter me. Dave, he 's been a-complainin' bekaze they wa'n't no salsody in the house, an' I rid over to Sue's to borry some. Airter I got thar,

Sue sez, se' she: 'Yess us pick up an' go an' light in on Puss,' se' she, 'an' fine out sump'n' nuther that's a-gwine on 'mongst folks,' se' she."

"Yes, lay it all onter me," said Mrs. Parmalee, looking over her spectacles at Mrs. Poteet; "I sez to Purithy, s' I, 'Purithy, yess go down an' see Puss,' s' I; 'maybe we 'll git a glimpse er that air new chap with the slick ha'r. Sid 'll be a-peggin' out airter awhile,' s' I, 'an' ef the new chap 's ez purty ez I hear tell, maybe I 'll set my cap fer 'im,' s' I."

At this fat Mrs. Puritha Hightower was compelled to lean on frail Mrs. Puss Poteet, so heartily did she laugh.

"I declar'," she exclaimed, "ef Sue hain't a sight! I 'm mighty nigh outdone. She 's thes bin a-gwine on that a-way all the time, an' I uv bin that tickled tell a little more an' I 'd a-drapped on the groun'. How 's all?"

"My goodness!" exclaimed Mrs. Poteet. "I hope you all know *me* too well to be a-stan'in' out there makin' excuse. Come right along in,

an' take off your things, an' ketch your win'.
Sis is home to-day."

"Well, I'm monstus glad," said Mrs. Hightower. "Sis useter think the world an' all er
me when she was a slip of a gal, but I reckon
she's took on town ways, hain't she? Hit ain't
nothin' but natchul."

"Sis is proud enough for to hol' 'er head
high," Mrs. Parmalee explained, "but she hain't
a bit stuck up."

"Well, I let you know," exclaimed Mrs. Hightower, untying her bonnet and taking off her
shawl, — "I let you know, here's what would n't
be sot back by nothin' ef she had Sis's chances.
In about the las' word pore maw spoke on 'er
dying bed, she call me to 'er an' sez, se' she,
'Purithy Emma,' se' she, 'you hol' your head
high; don't you bat your eyes to please none
of 'em,' se' she."

"I reckon in reason I oughter be thankful
that Sis ain't no wuss," said Mrs. Poteet, walking around with aimless hospitality; "yit that
chile's temper is powerful tryin', an' Teague

ackshully an' candidly b'leeves she 's made out'n
pyo' gol'.* I wish I may die ef he don't."

After awhile Sis made her appearance, buoy-
ant and blooming. Her eyes sparkled, her
cheeks glowed, and her smiles showed beautiful
teeth, — a most uncommon sight in the Mountains, where the girls were in the habit of rubbing snuff or smoking. The visitors greeted
her with the effusive constraint and awkward-
ness that made so large a part of their lives;
but after awhile Mrs. Hightower laid her fat,
motherly hand on the girl's shoulder, and looked
kindly but keenly into her eyes.

" Ah, honey ! " she said, " you hain't sp'ilt
yit, but you wa'n't made to fit thish here hill, —
that you wa'n't, *that* you wa'n't ! "

Women are not hypocrites. Their little
thrills and nerve convulsions are genuine while
they last. Fortunately for the women themselves, they do not last, but are succeeded by
others of various moods, tenses, and genders.
These nerve convulsions are so genuine and so

* Pure gold.

apt, that they are known as intuitions, and under this name they have achieved importance Mrs. Hightower, with all her lack of experience, was capable of feeling that Sis Poteet needed the by-no-means insubstantial encouragement that lies in one little note of sympathy, and she was not at all astonished when Sis responded to her intention by giving her a smart little hug.

Presently Mrs. Parmalee, who had stationed herself near the door, lifted her thin right arm and let it fall upon her lap.

" Well, sir!" she exclaimed, "ef yander ain't Sis's bo!"

Sis ran to the door, saw Woodward coming up the road, and blushed furiously,—a feat which Mrs. Hightower and Mrs. Parmalee, with all their experience, had rarely seen performed in that region.

Woodward greeted Mrs. Poteet's visitors with a gentle deference and an easy courtesy that attracted their favor in spite of themselves. Classing him with the "Restercrats," these women took keen and suspicious note of every

word he uttered and every movement he made,
holding themselves in readiness to become mor-
tally offended at a curl of the lip or the lifting
of an eyebrow; but he was equal to the occasion. He humored their whims and eccentri-
cities to the utmost, and he was so thoroughly
sympathetic, so genial, so sunny, and so handsome withal, that he stirred most powerfully the
maternal instincts of those weather-beaten bosoms and made them his friends and defenders.
He told them wonderful stories of life in the
great world that lay far beyond Hog Mountain,
its spurs and its foot-hills. He lighted their
pipes, and even filled them out of his own
tobacco pouch, a proceeding which caused Mrs.
Parmalee to remark that she "would like man-
nyfac'* mighty well ef 't wer' n't so powerful
weak."

Mrs. Hightower found early opportunity to
deliver her verdict in Sis's ear, whereupon the
latter gave her a little hug and whispered, —

---

* "Manufactured" tobacco, in contradistinction to the natural leaf.

"Oh, I just think he's adorable!" It was very queer, however, that as soon as Sis was left to entertain Mr. Woodward (the women making an excuse of helping Puss about dinner), she lost her blushing enthusiasm and became quite cold and reserved. The truth is, Sis had convinced herself some days before that she had the right to be very angry with this young man, and she began her quarrel, as lovely woman generally does, by assuming an air of tremendous unconcern. Her disinterestedness was really provoking.

"How did you like Sue Fraley's new bonnet last Sunday?" she asked, with an innocent smile.

"Sue Fraley's new bonnet!" exclaimed Woodward, surprised in the midst of some serious reflections; "why, I did n't know she had a new bonnet."

"Oh! you *did n't?* You were right *opposite.* I should think *anybody* could see she had a new bonnet by the way she tossed her head."

"Well, I did n't notice it, for one. Was it

one of these sky-scrapers? I was looking at
something else."

" *Oh!* "

Woodward had intended to convey a very
delicately veiled compliment, but this young
woman's tone rather embarrassed him. He
saw in a moment that she was beyond the
reach of the playful and ingenious banter
which he had contrived to make the basis of
their relations.

"Yes," he said, "I was looking at something
else. I had other things to think about."

"Well, she *did* have a new bonnet, with
yellow ribbons. She looked handsome. I hear
she's going to get married soon."

"I'm glad to hear it. She's none too young,"
said Woodward.

At another time Sis would have laughed
at the suggestion implied in this remark, but
now she only tapped the floor gently with her
foot, and looked serious.

"I hope you answered her note," she said
presently.

"What note?" he asked, with some astonishment.

Sis was the picture of innocence.

"Oh, I did n't think!" she exclaimed. "I
reckon it's a great *secret.* I mean the note
she handed you when she came out of church.
It's none of *my* business."

"Nor of mine, either," said Woodward, with a
relieved air. "The note was for Tip Watson."

This statement, which was not only plausible,
but true, gave a new direction to Sis's anger.

"Well, I don't see how anybody that thinks
anything of himself could be a mail-carrier
for *Sue Fraley*," she exclaimed scornfully;
whereupon she flounced out, leaving Woodward
in a state of bewilderment.

He had not made love to the girl, princi-
pally because her moods were elusive and
her methods unique. She was dangerously
like other women of his acquaintance, and
dangerously unlike them. The principal of
the academy in Gullettsville — a scholarly
old gentleman from Middle Georgia, who had

been driven to teaching by dire necessity —
had once loftily informed Woodward that Miss
Poteet was superior to her books, and the
young man had verified the statement to his
own discomfiture. She possessed that feminine
gift which is of more importance to a woman
in this world than scholarly acquirements,—
aptitude. Even her frankness — perfectly dis-
creet — charmed and puzzled Woodward; but
the most attractive of her traits were such as
mark the difference between the bird that
sings in the tree and the bird that sings in
the cage, — delightful, but indescribable.

When Sis Poteet began to question him
about Sue Fraley, the thought that she was
moved by jealousy gave him a thrill that was
new to his experience; but when she flounced
angrily out of the room because he had con-
fessed to carrying a note from Miss Fraley to
Tip Watson, it occurred to him that he might
be mistaken. Indeed, so cunning does mascu-
line stupidity become when it is played upon
by a woman that he frightened himself with

the suggestion that perhaps, after all, this perfectly original young lady was in love with Tip Watson.

During the rest of the day Woodward had ample·time to nurse and develop his new theory; and the more he thought it over, the more plausible it seemed to be. It was a great blow to his vanity; but the more uncomfortable it made him, the more earnestly he clung to it.

Without appearing to avoid him, Sis managed to make the presence of Mrs. Parmalee and Mrs. Hightower an excuse for neglecting him. She entertained these worthy ladies with such eager hospitality that when they aroused themselves to the necessity of going home, they found, to their dismay, that it would be impossible, in the language of Mrs. Poteet, to "git half-way acrost Pullium's Summit 'fore night 'ud ketch 'em." Sis was so delighted, apparently, that she became almost hilarious; and her gayety affected all around her except Woodward, who barely managed to conceal his disgust.

After supper, however, Mrs. Poteet and her

two guests betook themselves to the kitchen, where they rubbed snuff and smoked their pipes, and gossiped, and related reminiscences of that good time which, with old people, is always in the past. Thus Woodward had ample opportunity to talk with Sis. He endeavored, by the exercise of every art of conversation and manner of which he was master, to place their relations upon the old familiar footing, but he failed most signally. He found it impossible to fathom the gentle dignity with which he was constantly repulsed. In the midst of his perplexity, which would have been either pathetic or ridiculous if it had not been so artfully concealed, he managed for the first time to measure the depth of his love for this exasperating but charming creature whom he had been patronizing. She was no longer amusing; and Woodward, with the savage inconsistency of a man moved by a genuine passion, felt a tragic desire to humble himself before her.

"I'm going home to-morrow, Miss Sis," he said, finally, in sheer desperation.

"Well, you 've had a heap of fun — I mean," she added, "that you have had a nice time."

"I have been a fool!" he exclaimed bitterly. Seeing that she made no response, he continued: "I 've been a terrible fool all through. I came here to hunt up blockade whiskey — "

"*What!*"

Sis's voice was sharp and eager, full of doubt, surprise, and consternation.

"I came to Gullettsville," he went on, "to hunt up blockade whiskey and failed, and three weeks ago I sent in my resignation. I thought I might find a gold mine on my land-lot, but I have failed ; and now I am going to sell it. I have failed in everything."

Gloating over his alleged misfortunes, Woodward, without looking at Sis Poteet, drew from his pocket a formidable-looking envelope, unfolded its contents leisurely, and continued, —

"Even my resignation was a failure. Hog Mountain will be raided to-morrow or next day."

Sis rose from her chair, pale and furious, and

advanced toward him as if to annihilate him
with her blazing eyes. Such rage, such contempt, he had never before beheld in a woman's
face. He sat transfixed. With a gesture almost
tragic in its vehemence, the girl struck the papers from his hands.

"Oh, you mean, sneaking wretch! You —"
And then, as if realizing the weakness of
mere words, she turned and passed swiftly from
the room. Woodward was thoroughly aroused.
He was not used to the spectacle of a woman
controlled by violent emotions, and he recognized, with a mixture of surprise and alarm, the
great gulf that lay between the rage of Sis
Poteet and the little platitudes and pretences
of anger which he had seen the other women
of his acquaintance manage with such pretty
daintiness.

As the girl passed through the kitchen, she
seized a horn that hung upon the wall and ran
out into the darkness. The old women continued their smoking, their snuff-rubbing, and
their gossiping. Mrs. Hightower was giving

the details of a local legend showing how and why Edny Favers had " conjured " Tabithy Cozby, when suddenly Mrs. Poteet raised her hands, —

"*Sh-h-h !* "

The notes of a horn — short, sharp, and strenuous — broke in upon the stillness of the night. Once, twice, thrice! once, twice, thrice! once, twice, thrice! It was an alarm that did not need to be interpreted to the sensitive ear of Hog Mountain. The faces of the old women became curiously impassive. The firelight carried their shadows from the floor to the rafters, where they seemed to engage in a wild dance, — whirling, bowing, jumping, quivering; but the women themselves sat as still as statues. They were evidently waiting for something. They did not wait long. In a little while the sharp notes of the horn made themselves heard again, — once, twice, thrice ! once, twice, thrice ! once, twice, thrice !

Then the old women arose from their low chairs, shook out their frocks, and filed into the room where Mr. Philip Woodward, late of the revenue service, was sitting. There would have been a good deal of constraint on both sides; but before there could be any manifestation of this sort, Sis came in. She seemed to be crushed and helpless, nay, even humiliated.

"Why, my goodness, Sis!" exclaimed Mrs. Hightower, "you look natchully fagged out. A body 'ud think you 'd bin an' taken a run up the mountain. We all 'lowed you wuz in here lookin' airter your comp'ny. Wher' 'd you git the news?"

"From this gentleman here," Sis replied, indicating Woodward without looking at him. She was pale as death, and her voice was low and gentle.

Woodward would have explained, but the apparent unconcern of the women gave him no opportunity.

"I declare, Sis," exclaimed her mother, with a fond, apologetic little laugh; "ef you hain't a plum sight, I hain't never seed none."

"She's thes es much like her Gran'pap

7

Poteet," said Mrs. Hightower, " ez ef he 'd 'a' spit 'er right out'n his mouth, — that she is."

This led to a series of reminiscences more or less entertaining, until after awhile Sis, who had been growing more and more restless, rose and said, —

" Good-night, folks; I'm tired and sleepy. The clock has struck eleven."

" Yes," said Mrs. Poteet, " an' the clock's too fast, bekaze it hain't skacely bin mor'n a minnit sence the chickens crowed for ten."

This remark contained the essence of hospitality, for it was intended to convey to Mrs. Poteet's guests the information that if they were not ready to retire, she was prepared to discredit her clock in their interests. But there was not much delay on the part of the guests. The women were dying to question Sis, and Woodward was anxious to be alone; and so they said " Good-night," the earnestness and quaint simplicity of the old women carrying Woodward back to the days of his childhood, when his grandmother leaned tenderly over his little bed and whispered, "Good-night, dear heart, and pleasant dreams."

Shortly afterward the lights were put out, and, presumably, those under Teague Poteet's roof addressed themselves to slumber. But what of the news that Sis had given to the winds? There was no slumber for it until it had fulfilled its mission. Where did it go, and what was its burden? Three sharp blasts upon a horn, thrice repeated; then an interval; then three more, thrice repeated. Up, up the mountain the signal climbed; now faltering, now falling, but always climbing; sending echoes before it, and leaving echoes behind it, but climbing, climbing; now fainting and dying away, but climbing, climbing, until it reached Pullium's Summit, the smallest thread of sound. Two men were sitting talking in front of a cabin. The eldest placed one hand upon the shoulder of his companion, and flung the other to his ear. Faint and far, but clear and strenuous, came the signal. The men listened even after it had died away. The leaves of the tall chestnuts whipped each other gently, and the breeze that had borne the signal seemed to stay in the tops of the mountain pines as if awaiting further orders; and it had not long to wait.

The man who had held his hand to his ear slapped his companion on the back and cried, " Poteet's ! " and that was news enough for the other, who rose, stretched himself lazily, and passed into the cabin. He came out with a horn,— an exaggerated trumpet made of tin, — and with this to his lips he repeated to the waiting breeze, and to the echoes that were glad to be aroused, the news that had come from Poteet's. Across the broad plateau of Pullium's Summit the wild tidings flew until, reaching the western verge of the mountain, they dived down into Prather's Mill Road,— a vast gorge, so called because of the freak of a drunken mountaineer, who declared he would follow the stream that rushed through it until he found a mill, and was never heard of again.

The news from Poteet's was not so easily lost. It dropped over the sheer walls of the chasm, three hundred feet down, and refused to be drowned out by the rush and roar of the waters, as they leaped over the bowlders, until it had accomplished its mission. For here in Prather's Mill Road burned the slow fires that kept the Government officials in Atlanta at a white heat. They were burning now. If one of the officials could have crawled to the edge of the gorge, where everything seemed dwarfed by the towering walls of rock and the black abyss from which they sprang, he would have seen small fitful sparks of flame glowing at intervals upon the bosom of the deeper and blacker night below. These were the fires that all the power and ingenuity of the Government failed to smother, but they were now blown out one after another by the blasts from Sis Poteet's horn.

The news that was wafted down into the depths of Prather's Mill Road upon the wings of the wind was not at all alarming. On the contrary, it was received by the grimy watchers at the stills with considerable hilarity. To the most of them it merely furnished an excuse for a week's holiday, including trips to both Gullettsville and Villa Ray. Freely interpreted, it ran thus: "Friends and fellow-citizens: this is to inform you that Hog Mountain is to be raided by the revenue men by way of Teague Poteet's. Let us hear from you at once." There was neither alarm nor hurry, but the fires were put out quickly because that was the first thing to be done.

Teague Poteet owned and managed two stills. He was looking after some "doublings" when the notes of the horn dropped down into the gorge. He paused, and listened, and smiled. Uncle Jake Norris, who had come to have his jug filled, was in the act of taking a dram, but he waited, balancing the tin cup in the palm of his hand. Tip Watson was telling one of his stories to the two little boys who accompanied Uncle Jake, but it was never ended.

"Sis talks right out in meetin'," said Teague, after waiting to be sure there was no postscript to the message.

"What's the row, Teague?" asked Uncle Jake, swallowing his dram.

"'Nother raid comin' right in front er my door," Teague explained, "an' I reckon in reason I oughter be home when they go past. They useter be a kinder coolness betweenst me an' them revenue fellers, but we went to work an' patched it up."

Tip Watson appeared to be so overjoyed that he went through all the forms of a cotillon dance, imitating a fiddle, calling the figures, and giving his hand to imaginary partners. The boys fairly screamed with laughter at this exhibition, and Uncle Jake was so overcome that he felt called upon to take another dram, — a contingency that was renewed when Tip swung from the measure of a cotillon to that of a breakdown, singing, —

"I hain't bin a-wantin' no mo' wines — mo' wines —
Sence daddy got drunk on low wines — low wines."

"Come, Tip," said Teague, "yess shet up shop. Ef Sis ain't a caution," he said, after awhile, as he moved around putting things to rights. "Ef Sis ain't a caution, you kin shoot me. They hain't no mo' tellin' wher' Sis picked up 'bout thish 'ere raid than nothin' in the worl'. Dang me ef I don't b'lieve the gal's glad when a raid's a-comin'. Wi' Sis, hit's move *ment,* move*ment,* day in an' day out. They hain't nobody knows that gal less'n it's me. She knows how to keep things a-gwine. Some times she runs an' meets me, an' says, se' she : 'Pap, mammy's in the dumps; yess you an' me make out we er quollin'. Hit'll sorter stir 'er up;' an' then Sis, she'll light in, an' by the time we git in the house, she's a-scoldin' an' a-sassin' an' I'm a-cussin', an' airter awhile hit gits so hot an' natchul-like that I thes has ter drag Sis out behin' the chimbly and buss 'er to make certain an' shore that she ain't acci dentually flew off the han'le. Bless your soul an' body! she's a caution!"

"An' what's 'er maw a-doin' all that time?"

inquired Uncle Jake, as he took another dram with an indifferent air.

Teague laughed aloud as he packed the fresh earth over his fire.

" Oh, Puss! Puss, she thes sets thar a-chawin' away at 'er snuff, an' a-knittin' away at 'er socks tell she thinks I 'm a-pushin' Sis too clost, an' then she blazes out an' blows me up. Airter that," Teague continued, "things gits more home-like. Ef 't wa' n't fer me an' Sis, I reckon Puss 'ud teetotally fret 'erself away."

" St. Paul," said Uncle Jake, looking confidentially at another dram which he had poured into the tin cup, — " St. Paul says ther' er divers an' many wimmin, an' I reckon he know'd. Ther' er some you kin fret an' some you can't. Ther' 's my ole 'oman; more espeshually she 's one you can't. The livin' human bein' that stirs *her* up 'll have ter frail 'er out, er she 'll frail *him*."

" Well," said Teague, by way of condolence, " the man what 's stobbed by a pitchfork hain't much better off 'n the man that walks bar'-footed in a treadsaft patch."

The suggestion in regard to Mistress Norris seemed to remind Uncle Jake of something important. He called to his boys, took another modest dram, and disappeared in the undergrowth. Teague Poteet and his friends were soon ready to follow this worthy example, so that in another hour Prather's Mill Road was a very dull and uninteresting place from a revenue point of view.

II.

WOODWARD was aroused during the night by the loud barking of dogs, the tramp of horses, and the confused murmur of suppressed conversation. Looking from the window, he judged by the position of the stars that it was three or four o'clock in the morning. He sat upon the side of the bed and sought, by listening intently, to penetrate the mystery of this untimely commotion. He thought he recognized the voice of Tip Watson, and he was sure he heard Sid Parmalee's peculiar cough and chuckle. The conversation soon lifted itself out of the apparent confusion, and became comparatively distinct. The voices were those of Teague and Sis.

"Come now, pap, you must promise."

"Why, Sis, how *kin* I?"

" You shall, you shall, you *shall!* "

" Why, Sis, hon, he mought be a spy. Sid Parmalee he 'lows that the whole dad-blamed business is a put-up job. He wants to bet right now that we 'll all be in jail in Atlanty 'fore the moon changes. I lay they don't none of 'em fool Sid."

" You don't love me any more," said Sis, taking a new tack.

" Good Lord, Sis! Why, honey, what put that idee in your head? "

" I know you don't, — I know it! It 's always Dave Hightower this, and Sid Parmalee that, and old drunken Jake Norris the other. I just *know* you don't love me."

Teague also took a new tack, but there was a quiver in his voice born of deadly earnestness.

" I tell you, Sis, they er houndin' airter us; they er runnin' us down; they er closin' in on us; they er hemmin' us up. Airter they git your pore ole pappy an' slam 'im in jail, an' chain 'im down, who 's a-gwineter promise to take keer er *him?* Hain't ole man Joshway Blasingame bin sent away off to Al*benny?* Hain't ole man Cajy Shannon a-sarvin' out his time, humpback an' cripple ez he is? Who took keer er *them?* Who ast anybody to let up on 'em? But don't you fret, honey; ef they hain't no trap sot, nobody ain't a-gwineter pester *him.*"

"I wouldn't trust that Sid Parmalee out of my sight!" exclaimed Sis, beginning to cry. "I know him, and I know all of you."

"But ef they is a trap sot," continued Teague, ignoring Sis's tears, "*ef* they is, I tell you, honey, a thousan' folks like me can't hol' the boys down. The time's done come when they er teetotally wore out with thish 'ere sneakin' aroun' an' hidin'-out bizness."

This appeared to end the conversation, but it left Woodward considerably puzzled. Shortly afterward he heard a rap at his door, and before he could respond to the summons by inquiry or invitation, Teague Poteet entered with a lighted candle in his hand.

"I 'lowed the stirrin' 'roun' mought 'a' sorter rousted you," said Teague, by way of apology, as he placed the light on a small table and seated himself on a wooden chest.

"Yes. What's up?" Woodward inquired.

"Oh, the boys, — thes the boys," Teague replied, chuckling and rubbing his chin with an embarrassed air; "hit's thes the boys cuttin' up some er ther capers. They er mighty quare, the boys is," he continued, his embarrassment evidently increasing, "mighty quare. They uv up'd an' tuk a notion for to go on a little frolic, an' they uv come by airter me, an' nothin' won't do 'em but I mus' fetch you. S' I, 'Genter*men*, they hain't no manners in astin' a man on a marchin' frolic this time er night,' s' I; but Sid Parmalee, he chipped in an' 'lowed that you wuz ez high up for fun ez the next man."

Woodward thought he understood the drift of things, but he was desperately uncertain. He reflected a moment, and then faced the situation squarely.

"If you were in my place, Mr. Poteet, what would you do?" he asked.

This seemed to relieve Teague. His embarrassment disappeared. His eyes, which had been wandering uneasily around the room, sought Woodward's face and rested there. He took off his wide-brimmed wool hat, placed it carefully upon the floor, and ran his fingers through his iron-gray hair.

"I don't mind sayin'," he remarked grimly, "that I uv seed the time when I'd uv ast you to drap out'n that winder an' make for the bushes, knowin' that you'd tote a han'ful er bullets in thar wi' you. But on account er me an' Sis, I'm willin' to extracise my bes' judg*ment*. It may n't be satisfactual, but me and Sis is mighty long-headed when we pulls tergether. Ef I was you, I'd thes slip on my duds, an' I'd go out thar whar the boys is, an' I'd be high up for the'r frolic, an' I'd jine in wi' 'em, an' I'd raise any chune they give out."

With this Poteet gravely bowed himself out, and in a very few minutes Woodward was dressed and ready for adventure. He was young and bold, but he felt strangely ill at ease. He realized that, with all his address, he had never

been able to gain the confidence of these mountaineers, and he felt sure they connected him
with the revenue raid that was about to be made,
and of which they had received information.
He appreciated to the fullest extent the fact
that the situation called for the display of all
the courage and coolness and nerve he could
command; but, in the midst of it all, he longed
for an opportunity to show Sis Poteet the difference between a real man and a feeble-minded,
jocular rascal like Tip Watson.

His spirits rose as he stepped from the low
piazza into the darkness, and made his way to
where he heard the rattle of stirrups and spurs.
Some one hailed him, —

"Hello, Cap!"

"Ah-yi!" he responded. "It's here we go,
gals, to the wedding."

"I knowed we could count on 'im," said
the voice of Tip Watson.

"Yes," said Sid Parmalee, "I knowed it so
well that I fotch a extry hoss."

"Where are we going?" Woodward asked.

" Well," said Parmalee, " the boys laid off
for to have some fun, an' it's done got so these
times that when a feller wants fun he's got to
git furder up the mounting."

If the words were evasive, the tone was far
more so; but Woodward paid little attention to
either. He had the air of a man accustomed to
being called up in the early hours of the morning
to go forth on mysterious expeditions.

A bright fire was blazing in Poteet's kitchen,
and the light, streaming through the wide doorway, illuminated the tops of the trees on the
edge of the clearing. Upon this background
the shadows of the women, black and vast, —
Titanic indeed, — were projected as they passed
to and fro. From within there came a sound
as of the escape of steam from some huge engine;
but the men waiting on the outside knew that
the frying-pan was doing its perfect work.

The meat sizzled and fried; the shadows in
the tops of the trees kept up what seemed to
be a perpetual promenade, and the men outside waited patiently and silently. This silence

8

oppressed Woodward. He knew that but for his presence the mountaineers would be consulting together and cracking their dry jokes. In spite of the fact that he recognized in the curious impassiveness of these people the fundamental qualities of courage and endurance, he resented it as a barrier which he had never been able to break down. He would have preferred violence of some sort. He could meet rage with rage, and give blow for blow; but how was he to deal with the reserve by which he was surrounded? He was not physically helpless, by any means; but the fact that he had no remedy against the attitude of the men of Hog Mountain chafed him almost beyond endurance. He was emphatically a man of action, — full of the enterprises usually set in motion by a bright mind, a quick temper, and ready courage; but, measured by the impassiveness which these men had apparently borrowed from the vast, aggressive silences that give strength and grandeur to their mountains, how trivial, how contemptible, all his activities seemed to be!

But the frying was over after awhile. The Titanic shadows went to roost in the tops of the trees, and Teague Poteet and his friends, including ex-Deputy Woodward, took themselves and their fried meat off up the mountain, and the raid followed shortly after. It was a carefully planned raid, and deserved to be called a formidable one. Like many another similar enterprise it was a failure, so far as the purposes of the Government were concerned; but fate or circumstance made it famous in the political annals of that period. Fifteen men, armed with carbines, rode up the mountain. They were full of the spirit of adventure. They felt the strong arm of the law behind them. They knew they were depended upon to make some sort of demonstration; and this together with a dram too much here and there, made them a trifle reckless and noisy. They had been taught to believe that they were in search of outlaws. They caught from the officers who organized them something of the irritation which was the natural result of so many fruitless attempts to bring Hog Mountain to terms. They betrayed a sad lack of discretion. They brandished their weapons in the frightened faces of women and children, and made many foolish mistakes which need not be detailed here.

They rode noisily over the mountain, making a circle of Pullium's Summit, and found nothing. They peered over the precipitous verge of Prather's Mill Road, and saw nothing. They paused occasionally to listen, and heard nothing. They pounced upon a lonely pedler who was toiling across the mountain with his pack upon his back, and plied him with questions concerning the Moonshiners. This pedler appeared to be a very ignorant fellow indeed. He knew his name was Jake Cohen, and that was about all. He had never crossed Hog Mountain before, and, so help his gracious, he would never cross it again. The roads were all rough, and the ladies were all queer. As for the latter — well, great Jingo! they would scarcely look at his most beautiful collection of shawls and rib-

bons and laces, let alone buy them. In Villa
Ray (or, as Cohen called it, "Feel Hooray")
he had heard that Teague Poteet had been arrested and carried to Atlanta by a man named
Woodward. No one had told him this, but
he heard people talking about it wherever
he went in Villa Ray, and there seemed to
be a good deal of excitement in the settlement.

Cohen was a droll customer, the revenue officers thought; and the longer they chatted with
him the droller he became. First and last
they drew from him what they considered to be
some very important information. But most
important of all was the report of the arrest
of Teague Poteet. The deputies congratulated
themselves. They understood the situation
thoroughly, and their course was perfectly plain.
Poteet, in endeavoring to escape from them, had
fallen into the clutches of Woodward, and their
best plan was to overtake the latter before he
reached Atlanta with his prize, and thus share
in the honor of the capture. With this purpose

in view they took a dram all round and turned
their horses' heads down the mountain.

Cohen was indeed a droll fellow. He stood
in the road until the revenue men had disappeared. Then he unbuckled the straps of his
pack, dropped it upon the ground, and sat down
upon a bowlder. With his head between his
hands, he appeared to be lost in thought, but
he was only listening. He remained listening
until after the sounds of the horses' feet had
died away.

Then he carried his precious pack a little
distance from the roadside, covered it with
leaves, listened a moment to be sure that the
deputies were not returning, and then proceeded
to a little ravine in the side of the mountain
where the Moonshiners lay. He had been waiting nearly two days where the revenue men
found him, and his story of the capture of
Teague Poteet was concocted for the purpose
of sending the posse back down the mountain
the way they came. If they had gone on a
mile farther they would have discovered signs of

the Moonshiners, and this discovery would have
led to a bloody encounter, if not to the capture
of the leaders.

The deputies rode down the mountain in the
best of spirits. They had accomplished more
than any other posse ; they had frightened the
Moonshiners of Hog Mountain to their hiding-
places, and not a deputy had been killed or even
wounded. The clatter they made as they journeyed along attracted the attention of Ab
Bonner, a boy about fifteen, who happened to
be squirrel-hunting, and he stepped into the
road to get a good view of them. He was well
grown for his age, and his single-barrelled shot-
gun looked like a rifle. The revenue men
halted at once. They suspected an ambus-
cade. Experience had taught them that the
Moonshiners would fight when the necessity
arose, and they held a council of war. The
great gawky boy, with the curiosity of youth
and ignorance combined, stood in the road and
watched them. When they proceeded toward
him in a compact body, he passed on across

the road. Hearing a command to halt, he
broke into a run, and endeavored to make his
way across a small clearing that bordered the
road. Several of the deputies fired their guns
in the air; but one, more reckless than the rest,
aimed directly at the fugitive, and Ab Bonner
fell, shot through and through.

Viewed in its relations to all the unfortunate
events that have marked the efforts of the Government officials to deal with the violators of the
revenue laws from a political point of view, the
shooting of this ignorant boy was insignificant
enough. But it was important to Hog Mountain.
For a moment the deputy-marshals were stunned
and horrified at the result of their thoughtless-
ness. Then they dismounted and bore the boy
to the roadside again and placed him under the
shade of a tree. His blood shone upon the
leaves, and his sallow, shrunken face told a pitiful tale of terror, pain, and death.

The deputy-marshals mounted their horses
and rode steadily and swiftly down the mountain, and by nightfall they were far away. But

there was no need of any special haste. The winds that stirred the trees could carry no messages. The crows flying over, though they made a great outcry, could tell no tales. Once the boy raised his hand and cried, "Mammy!" but there was no one to hear him. And though ten thousand ears should listen, the keenest could hear him no more. He became a part of the silence — the awful, mysterious silence — that sits upon the hills and shrouds the mountains.

This incident in the tumultuous experience of Hog Mountain — the killing of Ab Bonner was merely an incident — had a decisive effect upon the movements of ex-Deputy Woodward. When Jake Cohen succeeded in turning the revenue officials back, the mountaineers made themselves easy for the day and night, and next morning prepared to go to their homes. Some of them lived on one side of Hog Mountain, and some on the other. They called themselves neighbors, and yet they lived miles apart; and it so happened that, with few exceptions, each

went in a different direction. Teague Poteet
gave the signal.

"Come, Cap," he said to Woodward, "yess
be a-traipsin'. Puss'll be a-puttin' on biskits
for supper before we git thar ef we don't push
on. Be good to yourse'f, boys, an' don't raise
no fracas."

Poteet and Woodward rode off together. That
afternoon, half a mile from Poteet's they met a
woman running in the road, crying and wringing
her hands wildly. She moved like one distracted. She rushed past them crying, —

"They uv killed little Ab! They uv killed
him. Oh, Lordy! they uv killed little Ab!"

She ran up the road a little distance and then
came running back; she had evidently recognized Poteet. As she paused in the road near
them, her faded calico sun-bonnet hanging upon
her shoulders, her gray hair falling about her
face, her wrinkled arms writhing in response
to a grief too terrible to contemplate, she seemed
related in some vague way to the prophets of
old who were assailed by fierce sorrows. Here

was something more real and more awful than death itself. Woodward felt in his soul that the figure, the attitude, the misery, of this poor old woman were all biblical.

"Oh, Teague," she cried, "they uv killed him! They uv done killed my little Ab! Oh, Lordy! that mortal hain't a-livin' that he ever done any harm. What did they kill him for?" Then she turned to Woodward: "Oh, Mister, Mister! *please* tell me what he done. *I'm* the one that made the liquor, *I'm* the one. Oh, Lordy! what did they kill little Ab for?"

Teague Poteet dismounted from his horse, took the woman firmly but gently by the arm, and made her sit down by the side of the road. Then, when she was more composed, she told the story of finding her son's body. It was a terrible story to hear from the lips of the mother, but she grew quieter after telling it, and presently went on her way. The two men watched her out of sight.

"I'll tell you what, Cap," said Teague, as he flung himself into the saddle, "they er houndin'

airter us. They er 'busin' the wimmin an' killin'
the childern; stidder carryin' out the law, they
er gwine about a-shootin' an' a-murderin'. *So
fur, so good.* Well, now, lem me tell you: the
hawk's done lit once too much in the chicken-
lot. This is a free country. I hain't a-layin'
no blame on you. Me and Sis stood by you
when the boys s'ore they wuz a-gwine to rattle
you up. We made 'em behave the'rse'ves, an'
I hain't a-blamin' you, but they er houndin' airter
us, an' ef I wuz you, I would n't stay on this
hill nary 'nuther minnit longer than it 'ud take
me to git off'n it. When the boys git wind er
this ongodly bizness, they ull be mighty hard to
hol'. I reckon maybe you 'l' be a-gwine down
about Atlanty. Well, you thes watch an' see
what stan' the Govern*ment*'s gwineter take 'bout
Ab Bonner; an' ef hit don't take no stan', you
thes drap in thar an' tell 'em how you seed a
ole man name Teague Poteet, an' *he* 'lowed that
the revenue fellers better not git too clost ter
Hog Mountain, bekaze the hidin'-out bizness is
done played. The law what's good enough fer

pore little Ab Bonner is good enough fer the men what shot 'im."

They rode on until they came to Poteet's house.

"We'll thes go in an' git a snack," said Teague, "an' airter that your best gait is a gallop."

But Woodward declined. He was dazed as well as humiliated, and he had no desire to face Sis Poteet. He pictured to himself the scorn and bitterness with which she would connect his presence on the Mountain with the murder of Ab Bonner, and he concluded to ride on to Gullettsville. He took Teague Poteet by the hand.

"Good-by, old man," he said; "I shall remember you. Tell Miss Sis — well, tell Miss Sis good-by." With that he wheeled his horse and rode rapidly toward Gullettsville.

It was a fortunate ride for him, perhaps. The wrath of Hog Mountain was mightily stirred when it heard of the killing of Ab Bonner, and Woodward would have fared badly at its hands. The wrath of others was stirred also. The unfortunate affair took the shape of a political issue, and thus the hands of justice were tied. But all this is a matter of history, and need not be dwelt upon.

In the meantime, as the days passed, Teague Poteet became dimly and uncomfortably conscious that a great change had come over Sis. One day she would be as bright and as gay as the birds in the trees; the next, she would be quiet, taciturn, and apparently depressed. As Teague expressed it, "One minnit hit's Sis, an' the nex' hit's some un else." Gradually the fits of depression grew more and more frequent and lasted longer. She was abstracted and thoughtful, and her petulance disappeared altogether. The contrast resulting from this change was so marked that it would have attracted the attention of a person of far less intelligence than Teague Poteet. He endeavored to discuss the matter with his wife, but Puss Poteet was not the woman to commit herself. She was a Mountain Sphinx.

"I'm afeard Sis is ailin'," said Teague, upon one occasion.

"Well," replied Puss, "she ain't complainin'."

"That's hit," Teague persisted; "she hain't complainin'. That's what pesters me. She looks lonesome, an' she's got one er them kinder fur-away looks in her eyes that gives me the all-overs." The Sphinx rubbed its snuff and swung in its rocking-chair. "Some days she looks holp up, an' then ag'in she looks cas' down. I 'low'd maybe you mought know what ailed her."

"Men folks," said Puss, manipulating her snuff-swab slowly and deliberately, "won't never have no sense while the worl' stan's. Ef a 'oman ain't gwine hether an' yan', rippity-clippity, day in an' day out, an' half the night, they er on the'r heads. Wimmen hain't men."

"That's so," replied Teague, gravely, "they hain't. Ef they wuz, the men 'ud be in a mighty nice fix."

"They'd have some sense," said Puss.

"Likely so. Yit 'oman er man kin shet one eye an' tell that Sis looks droopy; an' when Sis looks droopy I know in reason sump'n' nuther ails her."

"Well, goodness knows, I wish in my soul somebody'd shet one eye an' look at me," exclaimed Puss, with a touch of jealousy in her tone. "I traipse 'roun' this hill ontell I'm that wore out I can't drag one foot airter t'other, skacely, an' I don't never hear nobody up an' ast what ails *me*. It's Sis, Sis, Sis, all the time, an' eternally. Ef the calf's fat, the ole cow ain't got much choice betwixt the quogmire an' the tan-vat."

"Lord, how you do run on," said the iron-gray giant, rubbing his knuckles together sheepishly. "You don't know Sis ef you go on that away. Many's the time that chile 'ud foller me up an' say, 'Pap, ef you see my shawl a-hangin' out on the fence, Puss'll be asleep, an' don't you come a-lumberin' in an' wake her up, nuther.' An' many's the time she'd come out an' meet me, an' up an' say,

' Pap, Puss has taken an' bin a-mopin' all day long; yess you an' me go in an' fetch her up.' An', bless your life," Teague continued, addressing some imaginary person on the other side of the fireplace, " when me an' Sis sets our heads for to fetch anybody up, they er thes natchully erbleeged to come."

Puss rubbed her snuff and swayed to and fro in her rocking-chair, disdaining to make any reply to this array of facts and arguments; and Teague was as ignorant as ever of the cause of the queer change in his daughter. Perhaps, as becomes a dutiful husband, he should have retorted upon his complaining wife with complaints of his own; but his interests and his isolation had made him thoughtful and forbearing. He had the trait of gentleness which frequently sweetens and equalizes large natures. He remembered that behind whatever complaints — reasonable or unreasonable — Puss might make, there existed a stronghold of affection and tenderness; he remembered that her whole life had been

made up of a series of small sacrifices; he knew
that she was ready, whenever occasion made
it necessary, to cast aside her snuff-swab and
her complaints, and go to the rack without a
murmur.

But Teague was by no means satisfied with
the condition of affairs, so far as Sis was concerned. He said no more to his wife, but he
kept his eyes open. The situation was baf-
fling to the point of irritation, but Teague
betrayed neither uneasiness nor restlessness.
He hung about the house more, and he would
frequently walk in quietly when the women
thought he was miles away.

There were times when Sis ignored his presence altogether, but as a general thing she appeared to relish his companionship. Sometimes
at night, after her mother had gone to bed, she
would bring her chair close to Teague's, and
rest her head upon his shoulder, while he
smoked his pipe and gazed in the fire. Teague
enjoyed these occasions to the utmost, and
humored his daughter's slightest wish, respond-

ing to her every mood and fancy. If she talked, he talked; if she was silent, he said nothing. Once she dropped asleep with her head on his arm, and Teague sat holding her thus half the night. When she did awake she upbraided herself so earnestly for imposing on her old pappy (as she called him), that Teague yawned, and stretched himself, and rubbed his eyes, and pretended that he too had been asleep.

"Lordy, honey! I wuz that gone tell I did n't know whe'er I 'uz rolled up in a haystack er stretched out in a feather-bed. I reckon ef you 'd 'a' listened right clost you 'd 'a' heern me sno'. I thes laid back an' howled at the rafters, an' once-t er twice-t I wuz afeard I mout waken up Puss."

Sis's response to this transparent fib was an infectious peal of laughter, and a kiss which amply repaid Teague for any discomfort to which he may have been subjected.

Once, after Sis had nestled up against Teague, she asked somewhat irrelevantly, —

"Pap, do you reckon Mr. Woodward was a revenue spy after all?"

"Well, not to'rds the last. He drapped that business airter he once seed its whichaways. What makes you ast?"

"Because I hate and despise revenue spies."

"Well, they hain't been a-botherin' roun' lately, an' we hain't got no call to hate 'em tell they gits in sight. Hatin' is a mighty ha'sh disease. When Puss's preacher comes along, he talks ag'in it over the Bible, an' when you call 'im in to dinner, he talks ag'in it over the chicken-bones. I reckon hit's mighty bad, — mighty bad."

"Did you like him?"

"Who? Puss's preacher?"

"Now, you know I don't mean *him*, pap."

"*Oh!* Cap'n Woodward. Well, I tell you what, he had mighty takin' ways. Look in his eye, an' you would n't see no muddy water; an' he had grit. They hain't no two ways about that. When I ast 'im out with us that night, he

went like a man that had a stool to a quiltin'-
bee; an' when Duke Dawson an' Sid Parmalee
flung out some er the'r slurs, he thes snapt his
fingers in the'r face, an' ups an' says, says he,
' Gents, ef you er up for a frolic, I 'm your man,
an' ef you er in for a fight, thes count me in,'
says he. The boys wuz a little drinky," said
Teague, apologetically.

Sis squeezed up a little closer against her
father's shoulder.

" Did they fight, pap ? "

" Lord bless you, no. I thes taken an' flung
my han' in Duke's collar an' fetched 'im a
shake er two, an' put 'im in a good humor
thereckly; an' then airterwerds Tip Watson sot
'em all right when he read out the letter you
foun' on the floor."

" Oh, pap ! " Sis exclaimed in a horrified
tone, "I *slapped* that letter out of Mr. Woodward's *hand !*"

Teague laughed exultantly.

" What 'd he say ?"

" He did n't say *anything*. He looked like he

expected the floor to open and swallow him. I never was so ashamed in my life. I've cried about it a thousand times."

"Why, honey, I would n't take an' *cry* 'bout it ef I wuz you."

"Yes, you would, pap, if — if — you were me. I don't know what came over me; I don't know how I could be so hateful. No *lady* would ever do such a thing as that."

Sis gave her opinion with great emphasis. Teague took his pipe out of his mouth.

"Well, I tell you what, honey, they mought er done wuss. I let you know, when folks is got to be a-runnin' here an' a-hidin' yander, hit's thes about time for the gals for to lose the'r manners. Nobody would n't a-blamed you much ef you 'd a-fetched the Cap'n a clip stidder the letter; leastways, *I* would n't."

The girl shivered and caught her breath.

"If I had hit *him*," she exclaimed vehemently, "I should have gone off and killed myself."

"*Shoo!*" said Teague, in a tone intended to

be at once contemptuous and reassuring, but it was neither the one nor the other.

This conversation gave Teague fresh cause for anxiety. From his point of view, Sis's newly developed humility was absolutely alarming, and it added to his uneasiness. He recognized in her tone a certain shyness which seemed to appeal to him for protection, and he was profoundly stirred by it without at all understanding it. With a tact that might be traced to either instinct or accident, he refrained from questioning her as to her troubles. He was confused, but watchful. He kept his own counsel, and had no more conferences with Puss. Perhaps Puss was also something of a mystery; if so, she was old enough to take care of her own affairs.

Teague had other talks with Sis, — some general, some half-confidential, — and he finally became aware of the fact that every subject led to Woodward. He humored this, awkwardly but earnestly, and thought he had a clew; but it was a clew that pestered him more than ever.

He turned it round in his mind and brooded over it. Woodward was a man of fine appearance and winning manners, and Sis, with all the advantages — comparative advantages, merely — that the Gullettsville Academy had given her, was only a Mountain girl after all. What if — Teague turned away from the suspicion in terror. It was a horrible one; but as often as he put it aside, so often he returned to it. It haunted him. Turn where he might, go where he would, it pursued him night and day.

One mild afternoon in the early spring, Mr. Philip Woodward, ex-Deputy Marshal, leaned against the railing of Broad Street bridge in the city of Atlanta, and looked northward to where Kennesaw Mountain rises like a huge blue billow out of the horizon and lends picturesqueness to the view. Mr. Woodward was in excellent humor. He had just made up his mind in regard to a matter that had given him no little trouble. A wandering prospector, the agent of a company of Boston capitalists, had

told him a few hours before that he would be
offered twenty thousand dollars for his land-lot
on Hog Mountain. This was very important,
but it was not of the highest importance. He
nodded familiarly to Kennesaw, and thought:
" I 'll slip by you to-morrow and make another
raid on Hog Mountain, and compel that high-
tempered girl to tell me what she means by
troubling me so."

A train of cars ran puffing and roaring under
the bridge ; and as Woodward turned to follow
it with his eye he saw standing upon the other
side a tall, gaunt, powerful-looking man, whom
he instantly recognized as Teague Poteet.
Teague wore the air of awkward, recklessly
helpless independence which so often deceives
those who strike the Mountain men for a trade.
Swiftly crossing the bridge, Woodward seized
Teague and greeted him with a cordiality that
amounted to enthusiasm.

" Well, of all the world, old man, you are the
one I most wanted to see." Teague's thoughts
ran with grim directness to a reward that had

been offered for a certain gray old Moonshiner
who had made his head-quarters on Hog Mountain. "How are all at home?" Woodward
went on, "and what is the news?"

"The folks is porely and puny," Teague
replied, "an' the news won't b'ar relatin'
skacely. I hain't a-denyin'," he continued,
rubbing his chin and looking keenly at the
other, "I hain't a-denyin' but what I'm a-huntin'
airter you, an' the business I come on hain't got
much howdyin' in it. Ef you uv got some place
er nuther wher' ever'body hain't a-cockin' up
the'r years at us, I'd like to pass some words
wi' you."

"Why, of course," exclaimed Woodward,
hooking his arm in Teague's. "We'll go to my
room. Come! And after we get through, if
you don't say that my business with you is more
important than your business with me, then I'll
agree to carry you to Hog Mountain on my
back. Now that's a fair and reasonable proposition. What do you say?"

Woodward spoke with unusual warmth, and

there was a glow of boyish frankness in his tone and manners that Teague found it hard to resist.

"Well, they's thes this much about it," he said. "My business is mighty troublesome, an' yit hit's got to be settled up."

He had put a revolver in his pocket on account of this troublesome business.

"So is mine troublesome," responded Woodward, laughing, and then growing serious. "It has nearly worried me to death."

Presently they reached Woodward's room, which was up a flight of stairs near the corner of Broad and Alabama Streets. It was a very plain apartment, but comfortably furnished and kept with scrupulous neatness.

"Now, then," said Woodward, when Teague had seated himself, "I'll settle my business, and then you can settle yours." He had seated himself in a chair, but he got up, shook himself, and walked around the room nervously. The lithograph portrait of a popular burlesque actress stared brazenly at him from the mantelpiece. He took this remarkable work of art, folded it across the middle, and threw it into the grate. " I 've had more trouble than enough," he went on, " and if I had n't met you to-day I intended to hunt you up to-morrow."

" In Atlanty ? "

" No ; on Hog Mountain. Oh, I know the risk ! " Woodward exclaimed, misinterpreting Teague's look of surprise. " I know all about that, but I was going just the same. Has Miss Sis ever married ? " he asked, stopping before Teague and blushing like a girl.

" Not less'n it happened sence last We'n'sday, an' that hain't noways likely," replied the other, with more interest than he had yet shown. Woodward's embarrassment was more impressive than his words.

" I hardly know how to say it," he continued, " but what I wanted to ask you was this : Suppose I should go up to Hog Mountain some fine morning, and call on you and say, as the fellow did in the song, ' Old man, old man, give me your daughter,' and you should reply, ' Go upstairs and take her if you want to,' what do you suppose the daughter would say ? "

Woodward tried in vain to give an air of banter to his words. Teague leaned forward with his hands upon his knees.

"Do you mean would Sis marry you ? " he asked.

" That is just exactly what I mean," Woodward replied.

The old mountaineer rose and stretched himself, and drew a deep sigh of relief. His horrible suspicion had no foundation. He need not fly to the mountains with Woodward's blood upon his hands.

" Lem me tell you the honest truth, Cap," he said, placing his hand kindly on the young man's shoulder, " I might 'low she would, an' I might 'low she would n't; but I 'm erbleege to tell you that I dunno nothin' 'bout that gal no more 'n ef I had n't a-never seed 'er. Wimmin is mighty kuse."

" Yes," said Woodward, " they are curious."

" Some days they er gwine rippitin' aroun'
like the woods wuz a-fire, an' then ag'in they
er mopin' an' a-moonin' like ever' minnit wuz
a-gwine to be the nex'. I bin a-studyin' Sis
sence she wa'n't no bigger 'n a skinned rabbit,
an' yit I hain't got to A B C, let alone *a-b*
ab, *u-b* ub. When a man lays off for to keep
up wi' the wimmin folks, he kin thes make
up his min' that he 'll have to git in a dark
corner an' scratch his head many a time when
he oughter be a-diggin' for his livin'. They 'll
addle 'im thereckly."

" Well," said Woodward, with an air of de-
termination, " I 'm going back with you and
hear what Miss Sis has to say. Sit down.
Did n't you say you wanted to see me on business ? "

" I did start out wi' that idee," said Teague,
slipping into a chair and smiling curiously,
" but I disremember mostly what 't wuz about.
Ever'thing is been a-pesterin' me lately, an' a
man that 's hard-headed an' long-legged picks
up all sorts er foolish notions. I wish you 'd

take keer this pickle-bottle, Cap," he continued, drawing a revolver from his coat-tail
pocket and placing it on the table. " I uv
bin afeared ever sence I started out that the
blamed thing 'ud go off an' t'ar my jacket
wrong-sud-outerds. Gim me a gun, an' you 'll
gener'lly fin' me somewheres aroun'; but them
ar clickety-cluckers is got mos' too many holes
in 'em for to suit my eyesight."

Usually, it is a far cry from Atlanta to
Hog Mountain, but Teague Poteet and Woodward lacked the disposition of loiterers. They
shortened the distance considerably by striking
through the country, the old mountaineer re-
marking that if the big road would take care
of itself he would try and take care of himself.

They reached Poteet's one afternoon, cre-
ating a great stir among the dogs and geese
that were sunning themselves outside the
yard. Sis had evidently seen them coming,
and was in a measure prepared; but she
blushed painfully when Woodward took her

hand, and ran into her father's arms with a little hysterical sob.

" Sis did n't know a blessed word 'bout my gwine off to Atlanty," said Teague, awkwardly but gleefully. " Did you, honey ? "

Sis looked from one to the other for an explanation. Woodward was smiling the broad, unembarrassed smile of the typical American lover, and Teague was laughing. Suddenly it occurred to her that her father, divining her secret, — her sweet, her bitter, her well-guarded secret, — had sought Woodward out and begged him to return. The thought filled her with such shame and indignation as only a woman can experience. She seized Teague by the arm, —

" Pap, have you been to Atlanta ? "

" Yes, honey, an' I made 'as'e to come back."

" Oh, how could you ! How *dare* you do such a thing ! " she exclaimed passionately. " I will never forgive you as long as I live, — never ! "

" Why, honey — "

But she was gone, and neither Teague nor her mother conld get a word of explanation from her. Teague coaxed and wheedled and threatened, and Puss cried and quarrelled; but Sis was obdurate. She shut herself in her room and remained there. Woodward was thoroughly miserable. He felt that he was an interloper in some measure, and yet he was convinced that he was the victim of a combination of circumstances for which he was in no wise responsible. He had never made any special study of the female mind, because, like most young men of sanguine temperament, he was convinced that he thoroughly understood it; but he had not the remotest conception of the tragic element which, in spite of social training or the lack of it, controls and gives strength and potency to feminine emotions. Knowing nothing of this, Woodward knew nothing of women.

The next morning he was stirring early, but he saw nothing of Sis. He saw nothing of her during the morning, and at last, in the bitterness of his disappointment, he saddled his horse and made preparations to go down the mountain.

" I reckon it hain't no use to ast you to make out your visit," said Teague, gloomily. " That 's what I says to Puss. I 'm a free nigger ef Sis don't beat my time. You 'll be erbleege to stop in Gullettsville to-night, an' in case er accidents you thes better tie this on your coat."

The old mountaineer produced a small piece of red-woollen string and looped it in Woodward's button-hole.

" Ef any er the boys run up wi' you an' begin to git limber-jawed," Teague continued, " thes hang your thum' in that kinder keerless like, an' they 'll sw'ar by you thereckly. Ef any of 'em asts the news, thes say they 's a leak in Sugar Creek. Well, well, well ! " he exclaimed, after a little pause ; " hit 's thes like I tell you. Wimmin folks is mighty kuse."

When Woodward bade Puss good-by, she looked at him sympathetically and said, —

" Some time, when you er passin' by, I 'd be

mighty thankful ef you 'ud fetch me some maccaboy snuff."

The young man, unhappy as he was, was almost ready to accuse Mrs. Poteet of humor, and he rode off with a sort of grim desire to laugh at himself and the rest of the world. The repose of the Mountain fretted him; the vague blue mists that seemed to lift the valleys into prominence and carry the hills farther away, tantalized him; and the spirit of spring, just touching the great woods with a faint suggestion of green, was a mockery. There was a purpose — a decisiveness — in the stride of his horse that he envied, and yet he was inclined to resent the swift amiability with which the animal moved away.

But it was a wise steed; for when it came upon Sis Poteet standing by the side of the road, it threw up its head and stopped. Woodward lifted his hat, and held it in his hand. She gave him one little glance, and then her eyes drooped.

"I wanted to ask you something," she said,

pulling a dead leaf to pieces. Her air of humility was charming. She hesitated a moment, but Woodward was too much astonished to make any reply. "Are you very mad?" she asked with bewitching inconsequence.

"Why should *I* be mad, Miss Sis? I am glad you have given me the opportunity to ask your pardon for coming up here to worry you."

"I wanted to ask you if pap — I mean, if father went to Atlanta to see you," she said, her eyes still bent upon the ground.

"He said he wanted to see me on business," Woodward replied.

"Did he say anything about me?"

"Not that I remember. He never said anything about his business, even," Woodward went on. "I told him about some of my little troubles; and when he found I was coming back here, he seemed to forget all about his own business. I suppose he saw that I would n't be much interested in anybody else's business but my own just then."

Sis lifted her head and looked steadily at
Woodward. A little flush appeared in her
cheeks, and mounted to her forehead, and then
died away.

"Pap does n't understand — I mean he does
n't understand everything, and I was afraid he
had — Why do you look at me so?" she exclaimed, stopping short and blushing furiously.

"I ask your pardon," said the young man;
"I was trying to catch your meaning. You say
you were afraid your father — "

"Oh, I am not afraid now. Don't you think
the weather is nice?"

Woodward was a little puzzled, but he was
not embarrassed. He swung himself off his
horse and stood beside her.

"I told your father," he said, drawing very
near to the puzzling creature that had so wil-
fully eluded him, — "I told your father that I
was coming up here to ask his daughter to
marry me. What does the daughter say?"

She looked up in his face. The earnestness
she saw there dazzled and conquered her. Her

head drooped lower, and she clasped her hands together. He changed his tactics.

" Is it really true, then, that you hate me ? "

" Oh ! if you only knew ! " she cried, and with that Woodward caught her in his arms.

An hour afterwards, Teague Poteet, sitting in his low piazza, cleaning and oiling his rifle, heard the sound of voices coming from the direction of the Gullettsville road. Presently Sis and Woodward came in sight. They walked slowly along in the warm sunshine, wholly absorbed in each other. Woodward was leading his horse, and that intelligent animal improved the opportunity to nip the fragrant sassafras buds just appearing on the bushes. Teague looked at the two young people from under the brim of his hat and chuckled ; but when Sis caught sight of him, a little while after, he was rubbing his rifle vigorously, and seemed to be oblivious to the fact that two young people were making love to each other in full view. But Sis blushed all the same, and the blushes increased as she approached the house, until Woodward thought in his soul that her rosy shyness was the rarest manifestation of loveliness to be seen in all the wide world. As she hovered a moment at the gate, blushing and smiling, the old mountaineer turned the brim of his hat back from his eyes and called out with a great pretence of formal hospitality, —

"Walk in an' rest yourselves; thes walk right in! Hit 's lot's too soon in the season for the dogs to bite. Looks to me, Cap, like you hain't so mighty tender wi' that 'ar hoss er yourn. Ef you uv rid 'im down to Gullettsville an' back sence a while ago, he 'll be a needin' feed therreckly. Thes come right in an' make yourselves at home."

Woodward laughed sheepishly; but Sis rushed across the yard, flung her arms around Teague's neck and fell to crying with a vehemence that would have done credit to the most broken-hearted of damsels. The grizzled old mountaineer gathered the girl to his bosom and stroked her hair gently as he had done a thou-

sand times before. He looked at Woodward
with glistening eyes.

"Don't min' Sis, Cap. Sis hain't nothin' but
a little bit of a slip of a gal, an' sence the day
she could toddle 'roun' an' holler — good news
er bad, mad er glad — she 's bin a runnin' an'
havin' it out wi' her ole pappy. Wimmin an'
gals hain't like we-all, Cap; they er mighty
kuse. She never pestered wi' Puss much," continued Teague, as his wife came upon the scene,
armed with the plaintive air of slouchiness,
which is at once the weapon and shield of
women who believe that they are martyrs, —
"she never pestered wi' Puss much, but, cry or
laugh, fight or frolic, she allers tuck it out on
her pore ole pappy."

Puss asked no questions. She went and
stood by Teague, and toyed gently with one of
Sis's curls.

"Sis don't take airter none er the Pringles,"
she said after awhile, by way of explanation.
"They hain't never bin a day when I could n't
look at Teague 'thout battin' my eyes, an' Ma

use to say she 'uz thes that away 'bout Pap. I
never know'd what the all-overs wuz tell thes
about a hour before me an' Teague wuz married.
We uz thes about ready for to go an' face the
preacher, when Ma comes a-rushin' in — an' she
won't never be no paler when she 's laid out than
she wuz right that minnit. 'In the name er the
Lord, Ma, is you seed a ghost?' s' I. 'Puss!'
se' she, 'the cake hain't riz!' I thes tell you
what, folks, I like to a went through the floor, —
that I did!"

At this Sis looked up and laughed, and they all
laughed except Puss, who eyed Woodward with
an air of faint curiosity, and dryly remarked, —

"I reckon you hain't brung me my maccaboy snuff. I lay me an' my snuff wa'n't in
your min'. 'Let the old hen cluck,' ez the
sparrer-hawk said when he courted the pullet.
Well," she continued, smiling with genuine
satisfaction as she saw that Woodward no
more than half relished the comparison, "I
better be seein' about dinner. Ol' folks like
me can't live on love."

The days that followed were very happy
ones for the two young people — and for the
two old people for that matter. Teague enjoyed the situation immensely. He would
watch the young lovers from afar, and then go
off by himself and laugh heartily at his own
conceits. He was very proud that Sis was
going to marry Somebody, — a very broad term
as the old mountaineer employed it. At night
when they all sat around the fire (spring on
Hog Mountain bore no resemblance to summer), Teague gave eager attention to Woodward's stories and laughed delightedly at his
silliest jokes.

If Teague was pleased with Woodward,
he was astounded at Sis. She was no longer
the girl that her surroundings seemed to call
for. She was a woman, and a very delightful
one. From the old scholar whom fate or circumstance had sent to preside over the Gullettsville Academy, she had caught something
of the flavor and grace of cultivation, — a
gentle dignity, leaning always to artlessness,

and a quick appreciation, which was in itself a rare accomplishment.

The day for the wedding was set, and Woodward went his way to Atlanta. He had urged that the ceremony be a very quiet one; but Teague had different views, and he beat down all opposition.

"Why, good Lord, Cap!" he exclaimed, "what 'ud the boys say? Poteet's gal married an' no stools* give out! No, siree! Not much. We hain't that stripe up here, Cap. We hain't got no quality ways, but we allers puts on the pot when comp'ny comes. Me an' Sis an' Puss hain't had many weddin's 'mongst us, an' we 're thes a-gwine to try an' put the bes' foot foremos'. Oh, no, Cap! You fetch your frien's an' we 'll fetch our'n, an' ef the house hain't roomy enough, bless you! the woods is."

When Hog Mountain heard the news, which it did by special messenger, sent from house to house with little pink missives written by

* Invitations.

Sis, it was as proud as Teague himself. Fat
Mrs. Hightower laid aside her spectacles when
the invitation was translated to her, and remarked, —

"They hain't nobody on the face er the
yeth good enough fer Sis, but that air feller's
got the looks an' the spunk. I 'll set in this
very day an' hour, an' I 'll bake Sis a cake
that 'll make the'r eyes water." And so it
went. Everybody on Hog Mountain had some
small contributions to make.

The wedding, however, was not as boisterous as the boys proposed to make it. They
had their frolic, to be sure, as Sid Parmalee
or Tip Watson will tell you, but an incident
occurred which took the edge off their enjoy-
ment, and gave them the cue of soberness.

Two of Woodward's friends — young men
from Atlanta — bore him company to Hog
Mountain. At Gullettsville they fell in with
Uncle Jake Norris, at all times a jovial and
companionable figure.

"Roundabout man, roundabout way," re-

marked Uncle Jake, by way of explaining his
presence in Gullettsville. "My house is away
an' beyan' frum Poteet's, but I says to myself,
s'I, in obejunce to the naked demands of the
law I'll go this day an' git me a jug 'er licker
that's bin stomped by the govunment, an' hide
it an' my wickedness, ez you may say, in
Teague's hoss-stable. Yes, frien's, them wuz
the words. 'Let the licker be stomped by
the govunment for the sakes of the young
chap,' s'I, 'an' I'll hide the jug along er my
wickedness in Teague's hoss-stable.' So then,
frien's, yess be a sojourneyin', an' ef you feel the
needance er somethin' quick an' strong for to
brace you for enjorance, make your way to
the lot, an' feel behin' the stable-door — an'
watch out for the kickin' mule! I give you
my intentionals cle'r an' clean. What does
St. Paul say? 'Ef you can't do good by slip-
pance, do it by stealth.'"

They journeyed along as rapidly as the nature
of the mountain road would permit; but before
they reached Poteet's the shadows of twilight

began to deepen. The road, like most mountain roads, wound itself painfully about. At one point they were within a short half-mile of Poteet's, but a towering wall of rock barred their approach. The road, accommodating itself to circumstances, allowed the towering wall to drive it three miles out of the way. Uncle Jake Norris, turning readily to reminiscences, connected the precipitous shelf with many of the mysterious disappearances that had at various times occurred in army and revenue circles.

"Natur' built it," he said lightly, "an' a jaybird showed it to the boys. Teague, up thar, he 'lowed that a man wi' gray eyes an' a nimble han' could git on that rock an' lay flat of his belly an' disembowel a whole army. Them wuz his words,— disembowel a whole army."

While Uncle Jake was speaking, the travellers had passed beyond the wall; but the declivity on their left was still too steep to accommodate the highway, and so they rode along with the shadows of night on one side of them and pale symptoms of the day on the other.

Suddenly a thin stream of fire, accompanied by the sharp crack of a rifle, shot out of the side of the mountain straight at Woodward, and seemed, as one of his companions said afterwards, to pass through him. His horse shied with a tremendous lurch, and Woodward fell to the ground.

"He is shot!" cried one of the young men.

"What devil's work is this?" exclaimed Uncle Jake. "Cap, you ain't hurt, is you?"

Receiving no reply, for Woodward was stunned into semi-unconsciousness, Uncle Jake addressed himself to the bushes, —

"Come forth," he cried. "Jestify this deed!"

There was a moment's silence, but not a moment's inaction. Uncle Jake leaped from his horse, and, telling the frightened young men to look after Woodward, ran up the mountain side a quarter of a mile, placed his hands to his mouth, and hallooed three times in rapid succession. Then he heard Poteet's dogs bark, and he hallooed again. This time he was answered from above, and he turned and ran back to where he left Woodward.

When he got there he beheld a sight and heard words that made his blood run cold. Woodward was still lying upon the ground, but by his side was kneeling a gaunt and hollow-eyed woman. Her thin gray hair hung loose upon her shoulders and about her eyes, and the ragged sleeves of her gown fluttered wildly as she flung her bony arms in the air. She was uttering loud cries.

"Oh, Lordy! it's little Ab! I uv done killed little Ab over ag'in! Oh, my little Ab! It's your pore ole Mammy, honey! Oh, Mister! Make little Ab wake up an' look at his pore ole Mammy!"

The two young men from Atlanta were paralyzed with horror. When Uncle Jake Norris ran up the mountain to alarm Poteet, the witch-like figure of the woman sprang from the bushes and fell upon Woodward with a loud outcry. The whole occurrence, so strange, so unnatural, and so unexpected, stripped the young men of their power of reasoning; and if the rocks had opened and fiery flames issued forth, their astonishment and perplexity and terror could have been no greater.

But if they had been acquainted with the history of this wild-eyed woman, — if they had known that for weeks she had been wandering over the mountain bereft of reason, and seeking an opportunity to avenge with her own hands the murder of Ab Bonner, her son, — they would have been overcome by pity. Uncle Jake Norris understood at once that Ab Bonner's mother had shot Woodward, and he forgot to be merciful.

"Woe unto you, woman, ef you have done this deed! Woe unto you an' your'n, Rachel Bonner, ef you have murdered this innocent!"

"That he wuz innocent!" exclaimed the woman, swaying back and forth and waving her hands wildly. "The unborn babe wa'n't no innocenter than little Ab!"

"Woe unto you, Sister Bonner!" Uncle Jake went on, examining Woodward and speak-

11

ing more calmly when he found him breathing regularly. "Woe unto you and shame upon you, Sister Bonner, to do this deed of onjestifiable homicide, ez I may say. Let min' an' flesh rankle, but shed no blood."

"Oh, my little Ab! I uv kilt 'im ag'in!"

"You may well sesso, Sister Rachel Bonner," said Uncle Jake, turning Woodward over and examining him with the crude skill of an old soldier; "you may well sesso. Drap down where you is, an' call on the Lord not to give you over to a reprobate min' for to do the things that are unconvenient, ez St. Paul says. Let tribulation work patience, lest you git forsook of hope, Sister Rachel Bonner. Come, Cap," he went on, addressing himself to Woodward, "Teague 'll be a-drappin' on us thereckly, an' it twon't never do in the roun' worl' for to be a-makin' faces at 'im frum the groun'. Roust up, roust up."

Woodward did rouse up. In fact, his unconsciousness was only momentary; but he had been making a vain effort to trace his surroundings, disordered as they were by the wild cries of the woman, to a reasonable basis.

By the time he had been helped to his feet, and had discovered that the bullet from Mrs. Bonner's rifle had merely grazed the fleshy part of his shoulder, Teague and a number of his friends had arrived upon the scene. There was nothing to be said, nothing to be done, except to move up the mountain to Poteet's.

"Ah, pore woman!" exclaimed Uncle Jake. "Pore mizerbul creetur! Come wi' us, Sister Rachel Bonner, come wi' us. Ther's a warm place at Teague's h'a'th fer sech ez you."

The woman followed readily, keeping close to Woodward. To her distracted eyes he took the shape of her murdered son. Poteet was strangely reticent. His tremendous stride carried him ahead of the horses, and he walked with his head held down as if reflecting. Once he turned and spoke to Parmalee, —

"Oh, Sid!"

"Ah-yi?"

"Thes s'posen it had 'a' bin a man?"

" Good-bye, Mr. Man! "

It is not necessary to describe the marriage of Sis and Woodward, nor to recite here the beautiful folk-songs that served for the wedding music. As Mrs. Poteet remarked after it was all over, " they wer' n't a bobble from beginnin' to een' ; " and when the wedding party started down the mountain in the early hours of the morning to take conveyances at Gullettsville for the railroad station thirty miles away, Uncle Jake Norris was sober enough to stand squarely on his feet as he held Sis's hand.

" Ez St. Paul says, I prophesy in perportion to my faith. You all is obleege to be happy. Take keer of thish 'ere gal, Cap! "

Teague Poteet went down the mountain a little way, and returned after awhile like a man in a dream. He paused at a point that overlooked the valley and took off his hat. The morning breeze, roused from its sleep, stirred his hair. The world, plunging swiftly and steadily through its shadow, could not rid itself of a star that burned and quivered in the east.

It seemed to be another world toward which Sis was going.

An old woman, gray-haired, haggard, and sallow, who had been drawn from the neighborhood of Hog Mountain by the managers of the Atlanta Cotton Exposition to aid in illustrating the startling contrasts that the energy and progress of man have produced, had but one vivid remembrance of that remarkable display. She had but one story to tell, and, after the Exposition was over, she rode forty miles on horseback, in the mud and rain, to tell it at Teague Poteet's.

"I wish I may die," she exclaimed, flinging the corners of her shawl back over her shoulders, and dipping her clay pipe in the glowing embers, — "I wish I may die ef I ever see sech gangs an' gangs an' gangs of folks, an' ef I git the racket out'n my head by next Chris'mas, I 'll be mighty lucky. They sot me over ag'in the biggest fuss they could pick out, an' gimme a pa'r er cotton kyards. Here 's what kin kyard

when she gits her han' in, an' I b'leeve'n my
soul I kyarded 'nuff bats to thicken all the
quilts betwix' this an' Californy. The folks,
they 'ud come an' stan' an' star', an' then they
'ud go some'r's else ; an' then new folks 'ud
come, an' stan', an' star', an' go some'r's else.
They wuz jewlarkers thar frum ever'where's,
an' they lookt like they wuz too brazen to live
skacely. Not that I keer'd. No, bless you!
Not when folks is a-plumpin' down the cash
money. Not me! No, siree! I wuz a-settin'
thar one day a-kyardin' away, a-kyardin' away,
when all of a sudden some un retched down an'
grabbed me 'roun' the neck, an' bussed me right
here on the jaw. Now, I hain't a-tellin' you no
lie, I like to 'a' fainted. I lookt up, an' who do
you reckon it wuz ?"

"I bet a hoss," said Teague, dryly, "that Sis
wa' n't fur from thar when that bussin' wuz a-
gwine on."

"Who should it be *but* Sis!" exclaimed the
old woman, leaning forward eagerly as she
spoke. "Who else but Sis wuz a-gwine to grab

me an' gimme a buss right here on the jaw a-frontin' of all them jewlarkers? When I lookt up an' seen it twuz Sis, I thought in my soul she 'uz the purtiest creetur I ever laid eyes on. ' Well, the Lord love you, Sis,' s' I, ' whar' on the face er the yeth did you drap frum?' s' I. I ketched 'er by the arm an' helt 'er off, an' s' I, ' Ef I don't have a tale to tell when I git home, no 'oman never had none,' s' I. She took an' buss'd me right frontin' of all them jewlarkers, an' airter she 'uz gone, I sot down an' had a good cry. I sot right flat whar' I wuz, an' had a good cry."

And then the old woman fell to crying softly at the remembrance of it, and those who had listened to her story cried with her. And narrow as their lives were, the memory of the girl seemed to sweeten and inspire all who sat around the wide hearth that night at Teague Poteet's.

BLUE DAVE.

BLUE DAVE.

I.

THE atmosphere of mystery that surrounds the Kendrick Place in Putnam County is illusive, of course; but the illusion is perfect. The old house, standing a dozen yards from the roadside, is picturesque with the contrivances of neglect and decay. Through a door hanging loose upon its hinges the passer-by may behold the evidences of loneliness and gloom, — the very embodiment of desolation, — a void, a silence, that is almost portentous. The roof, with its crop of quaint gables, in which proportion has been sacrificed to an effort to attain architectural liveliness, is covered with a greenish-gray moss on the north side, and has long been given over to decay on all sides. The cat-squirrels that occa-

sionally scamper across the crumbling shingles
have as much as they can do, with all their nim-
bleness, to find a secure foothold. The huge
wooden columns that support the double veranda
display jagged edges at top and bottom, and no
longer make even a pretence of hiding their
grim hollowness. The well, hospitably placed
within arm's reach of the highway, for the bene-
fit of the dead and buried congregation that long
ago met and worshipped at Bethesda meeting-
house, is stripped of windlass, chain, and bucket.
All the outhouses have disappeared, if they ever
had an existence; and nothing remains to tell
the story of a flourishing era, save a fig-tree
which is graciously green and fruitful in season.
This fig-tree has grown to an extraordinary
height, and covers a large area with its canopy
of limbs and leaves, giving a sort of Oriental
flavor to the illusion of mystery and antiquity.
It is said of this fig-tree that sermons have been
preached and marriages solemnized under its
wide-spreading branches; and there is a vague
tradition to the effect that a duel was once

fought in its shadow by some of the hot-bloods. But no harm will come of respectfully but firmly doubting this tradition; for it is a fact, common to both memory and observation, that duels, even in the old days, when each and every one of us was the pink of chivalry and the soul of honor, were much rarer than the talk of them. Nevertheless, the confession may be made that without such a tradition a fig-tree surrounded by so many evidences of neglect and decay would be a tame affair indeed.

The house, with its double veranda, its tall chimneys, and its curious collection of gables, was built as late as 1836 by young Felix Kendrick, in order, as Grandsir Kendrick declared, to show that "some folks was as good as other folks." Whether Felix succeeded in this or not, it is impossible to gather from either local history or tradition; but there is no doubt that the house attracted attention, for its architectural liveliness has never to this day been duplicated in that region. In those days the Kendrick family was a new one, so to speak, but ambitious.

Grandsir Kendrick — a fatal title in itself — was a hatter by trade, who had come to Georgia in search of a precarious livelihood. He obtained permission to build him a little log hut by the side of a running stream; and, for a year or two, people going along the road could hear the snap and twang of his bow-string as he whipped wool or rabbit fur into shape. Some said he was from North Carolina; others said he was from Connecticut; but whether from one State or the other, what should a hatter do away off in the woods in Putnam County? Grandsir Kendrick, who was shrewd, close-fisted, and industrious, did what any sensible man would have done; he became an overseer. In this business, which required no capital, he developed considerable executive ability. The plantations he had charge of paid large profits to their owners, and he found his good management in demand. He commanded a large salary, and saved money. This money he invested in negroes, buying one at a time and hiring them out. He finally came to be the owner of seven or eight stout field hands; whereupon he bought two hundred acres of choice land and set himself up as a patriarch.

Grandsir Kendrick kept to his sober ways, continued his good management, and, in the midst of much shabbiness, continued to put aside money in the shape of negroes. He also reared a son who contrived somehow to have higher notions than his father. These notions of young Felix Kendrick were confirmed and enlarged by his marriage to the daughter of a Methodist circuit-rider. This young lady had been pinched by poverty often enough to know the value of economy, while the position of her father had given her advantages which the most fortunate young ladies of that day might have envied. In short, Mrs. Felix turned out to be a very superior woman in all respects. She was proud as well as pretty, and managed to hold her own with the element which Grandsir Kendrick sometimes dubiously referred to as "the quality." The fact that Mrs. Felix's mother was a Barksdale probably had something to do with her energy and tact; but whatever the cause of her popularity may have been, Grandsir Kendrick was very proud of his son's wife. He had no sympathy with, and no part in, her high notions; but their manifestation afforded him the spectacle of an experience entirely foreign to his own. Here was his son's wife stepping high, and compelling his son to step high. So far as Grandsir Kendrick was concerned, however, it was merely a spectacle. To the day of his death, he never ceased to higgle over a thrip, and it was his constant boast that in his own experience it had always been convenient to give prudence the upper hand of pride.

In 1850 the house was not showing many signs of decay, but young Mrs. Felix had become the Widow Kendrick, her daughter Kitty had grown to be a beautiful young woman, and her son Felix was a lad of remarkable promise. The loss of her husband was a great blow to Mrs. Kendrick. With all her business qualities, her affection for her family and her home was strongly marked, and her husband stood first as the head and centre of each. Felix Kendrick

died in the latter part of November, 1849, and
his widow made him a grave under the shadow
of a tree he had planted when a boy, and in full
view of her window. The obsequies were very
simple. A prayer was said, and a song was
sung ; that was all. But it was understood that
the funeral sermon would be preached at the
house by Mrs. Kendrick's brother, who was on
his way home from China, where he had been
engaged in converting (to use a neighborhood
phrase) the " squinch-eyed heathen."

The weeks went by, and the missionary
brother returned ; and one Sunday morning in
February it was given out at Bethesda that " on
the first Sabbath after the second Tuesday in
March, the funeral sermon of Brother Felix
Kendrick will be preached at the house by
Brother Garwood." On the morning of this
particular Sunday, which was selected because
it did not conflict with the services of the Bethesda congregation, two neighbors met in the
forks of the public road that leads to Rockville.
Each had come from a different direction. One

was riding and one was walking; and both were past the middle time of life.

"Well met, Brother Roach!" exclaimed the man on horseback.

"You've took the words from my mouth, Brother Brannum. I hope you are well. I'm peart myself, but not as peart as I thought I was, bekaze I find that the two or three miles to come is sticking in my craw."

"Ah, when it comes to that, Brother Roach," said the man on horseback, "you and me can be one another's looking-glass. Look on me and you'll see what time has done for you."

"Not so, Brother Brannum! Not so!" exclaimed the other. "There's some furrows on your forrud, and a handful of bird-tracks below your eyes that would ill become me; and I'm plumper in the make-up, you'll allow."

"Yes, yes, Brother Johnny Roach," said Brother Brannum, frowning a little; "but what of that? Death takes no time to feel for wrinkles and furrows, and nuther does plumpness stand in the way. Look at Brother Felix Ken-

drick, — took off in the very pulse and power
of his prime, you may say. Yet, Providence
permitting, I am to hark to his funeral to-
day."

" Why, so am I, — so am I," exclaimed Brother
Roach. " We seem to agree, Brother Brannum,
like the jay-bird and the joree, — one in the tree
and t' other on the ground."

Brother Brannum's grim sense of superiority
showed itself in his calm smile.

" Yet I 'll not deny," continued Brother Roach,
flinging his coat, which he had been carrying on
his arm, across his shoulder, " that sech discourses go ag'in the grain. It frets me in the
mind for to hear what thundering great men
folks git to be arter they are dead, though I hope
we may both follow suit, Brother Brannum."

" But how, Brother Johnny Roach ?"

" Why, by the grace of big discourses, Brother
Brannum. There's many a preacher could close
down the Bible on his hankcher and make our
very misdeeds smell sweet as innocence. It's
all in the lift of the eyebrow, and the gesticures

of the hand. So old Neighbor Harper says, and he's been a lawyer and a schoolmaster in his day and time."

"Still," said Brother Brannum, as if acknowledging the arguments, "I think Sister Kendrick is jestified in her desires."

"Oh, yes,— oh, yes!" replied Brother Roach, heartily; "none more so. Felix Kendrick's ways is in good shape for some preacher wi' a glib tongue. Felix was a good man; he wanted his just dues, but not if to take them would hurt a man. He was neighborly; who more so? And, sir, when you got to rastlin' wi' trouble, he'd find you and fetch you out. I only hope the Chinee preacher'll be jedgmatical enough for to let us off wi' the simple truth."

"They say," said Brother Brannum, "that he's a man full of grace and fire."

"Well, sir," said Johnny Roach, "if he but makes me disremember that I left the bay mar' at home, I'll thank him kindly."

"Mercy, Brother Roach," exclaimed Brother Brannum, taking this as a neighborly hint, "mount up here and rest yourself, whilst I stretch my legs along this level piece of ground."

"I'd thank you kindly, Brother Brannum, if you wouldn't so misjudge me. It's my will to walk; but if I git my limbs sot to the saddle here and now, they'd ache and crack might'ly when next I called upon 'em. I'll take the will for the deed, Brother Brannum."

Thus these neighbors jogged along to Felix Kendrick's funeral. They found a great crowd ahead of them when they got there, though they were not too late for the services; but the house was filled with sympathetic men and women, and those who came late were compelled to find such accommodations as the yard afforded; and these accommodations were excellent in their way, for there was the cool, green grass under the trees, and there were the rustic seats in the shadow of the fig-tree of which mention has been made.

Coming together, Brother Brannum and Brother Roach stayed together; and they soon found themselves comfortably seated under the fig-tree, — a point of view from which they could observe everything that was going on. Brother Brannum, who was a pillar of Bethesda church and extremely officious withal, seemed to regret that he had not arrived soon enough to find a place in the house near the preacher, but Brother Roach appeared to congratulate himself that he had been crowded out of ear-shot.

"We can set here," he declared in great good-humor, "and hear the singing, and then whirl in and preach each man his own sermon. I know better than the furrin preacher what 'd be satisfactual to Felix Kendrick. I see George Denham sailing in and out and flying around; and if the pinch comes, as come it must, Brother Brannum, we can up and ast George for to fetch us sech reports as a hongry man can stomach."

Brother Brannum frowned heavily, but made no response. Presently Brother Roach beckoned to the young man whom he had called George Denham. "Howdy, George! How is

Kitty Kendrick? Solemn as the season is, George, I lay 't would be wrong for to let Beauty pine."

The young man suppressed a smile, and raised his hands in protest.

"Uncle Johnny! to joke me at such a time! I shall go to-morrow and cut your mill-race, and you will never know who did it."

"Ah, George! if death changes a man no more 'n they say it does, little does Felix Kendrick need to be holp by these dismal takings-on. From first to last, he begrudged no man his banter. But here we are and yan 's the preacher. The p'int wi' me, George, is, how kin we-all setting on the back seats know when the preacher gits to his 'amen,' onless his expound-ance is too loud to be becoming?"

"Come, now, Uncle Johnny," said young Denham, "no winking, and I 'll tell you. I was talking to Miss Kitty just now, and all of a sudden she cried out, 'Why, yonder 's Uncle Johnny Roach, and he 's walking, too. Uncle Johnny must stay to dinner;' and Mrs. Ken-

drick says, 'Yes, and Brother Brannum, too.'
And so there you are."

"Well, sir," exclaimed Brother Roach, "Kitty
always had a piece of my heart, and now she
has it all."

"A likely young man, that George Denham,"
said Brother Brannum, as Denham moved towards the house.

"You never spoke a truer word, Brother
Brannum," said Brother Roach, enthusiastically.
"Look at his limbs, look at his gait, look at his
eye. If the world, the flesh, and the devil don't
freeze out his intents, you'll hear from that
chap. He's a-gitting high up in the law, and
where'll you find a better managed plantation
than his'n?"

What else Brother Roach said or might have
said must be left to conjecture. In the midst
of his eulogy on the living, the preacher in the
house began his eulogy of the dead. Those who
heard what he said were much edified, and those
who failed to hear made a decorous pretence of
listening intently. In the midst of the sermon

Brother Roach felt himself touched on the arm. Looking up, he saw that Brother Brannum was gazing intently at one of the gables on the roof. Following the direction of Brother Brannum's eyes, Brother Roach beheld, with astonishment not unmixed with awe, the head and shoulders of a powerfully built negro. The attitude of the negro was one of attention. He was evidently trying to hear the sermon. His head was bent, and the expression of his face was indicative of great good-humor. His shirt was ragged and dirty, and had fallen completely away from one arm and shoulder, and the billowy muscles glistened in the sun. While Brother Brannum and Brother Roach were gazing at him with some degree of amazement, an acorn dropped upon the roof from one of the tall oaks. Startled by the sudden noise, the negro glanced hurriedly around, and dropped quickly below the line of vision.

"Well, well, well!" exclaimed Brother Roach, after exchanging a look of amazement with Brother Brannum. "Well, well, well! Who'd 'a' thought it. Once 't was the nigger in the woodpile; now it's the nigger in the steeple, and arter awhile they 'll be a-flying in the air, — mark my words. I call that the impidence of the Old Boy. Maybe you don't know that nigger, Brother Brannum?"

"I disremember if I do, Brother Roach."

"Well, sir, when one of 'em passes in front of your Uncle Johnny, you may up and sw'ar his dagarrytype is took. That nigger, roosting up there so slick and cool, is Bledser's Blue Dave. Nuther more, nuther less."

"Bledser's Blue Dave!" exclaimed Brother Brannum in a voice made sepulchral by amazement.

"The identical nigger! I'd know him if I met him arm-in-arm with the King and Queen of France."

"Why, I thought Blue Dave had made his disappearance five year ago," said Brother Brannum.

"Well, sir, my two eyes tells me different. Time and time ag'in I've been told he's a

quare creetur. Some say he's strong as a horse
and venomous as a snake. Some say he's
swifter than the wind and slicker than a red
fox. And many's the time by my own h'a'th-
stone I've had to pooh-pooh these relations;
yet there's no denying that for mighty nigh
seven year that nigger's been trolloping round
through the woods foot-loose and scotch-free,
bidding defiance to the law of the State and
Bill Brand's track dogs."

"Well, sir," said Brother Brannum, fetching
his hand down on his knee with a thwack, "we
ought to alarm the assemblage."

"Jes so," replied Brother Roach, with something like a chuckle; "but you forget the time
and the occasion, Brother Brannum. I'm a
worldly man myself, as you may say, but 't will
be long arter I'm more worldlier than what I
am before you can ketch me cuttin' sech a scol-
lop as to wind up a funeral sermon wi' a race
arter a runaway nigger."

Brother Brannum agreed with this view, but
it was with a poor grace. He had a vague re-

membrance of certain rewards that had from time to time been offered for the capture of Blue Dave, and he was anxious to have a hand in securing at least a part of these. But he refrained from sounding the alarm. With Brother Roach, he remained at the Kendrick Place after the sermon was over, and took dinner. He rode off shortly afterwards, and the next day Bill Brand and his track dogs put in an appearance; but Blue Dave was gone.

It was a common thing to hear of fugitive negroes; but Blue Dave (so called because of the inky blackness of his skin) had a name and a fame that made him the terror of the women and children, both white and black; and Kitty Kendrick and her mother were not a little disturbed when they learned that he had been in hiding among the gables of their house. The negro's success in eluding pursuit caused the ignorant-minded of both races to attribute to him the possession of some mysterious power. He grew into a legend; he became a part of the folk-lore of the section. According to popular belief, he possessed strange powers and great courage; he became a giant, a spirit of evil. Women frightened their children into silence by calling his name, and many a youngster crept to bed in mortal fear that Blue Dave would come in the night and whisk him away into the depths of the dark woods. Whatever mischief was done was credited to Blue Dave. If a horse was found in the lot spattered with mud, Blue Dave had ridden it; if a cow was crippled, a hog missing, or a smoke-house robbed, Blue Dave was sure to be at the bottom of it all, so far as popular belief was concerned. The negroes had many stories to tell of him. One had seen him standing by a tall poplar-tree. He was about to speak to him when there came a flash of lightning and a crash of thunder, and Blue Dave disappeared, leaving a sulphurous smell behind him. He had been seen by another negro. He was standing in the middle of the Armour's Ferry road. He was armed with a gleaming reap-hook, and accompanied by a big black dog. As soon as the dog saw the new-comer, it bristled up from head to foot, its eyes shone like two coals of fire, and every hair on its back emitted a fiery spark.

Very little was known of the history of Blue Dave. He was brought to the little village of Rockville in chains in a speculator's train, — the train consisting of two Conestoga wagons and thirty or forty forlorn-looking negroes. The speculator explained that he had manacled Blue Dave because he was unmanageable; and he put him on the block to sell him after making it perfectly clear to everybody that whoever bought the negro would get a bad bargain. Nevertheless Blue Dave was a magnificent specimen of manhood, straight as an arrow, as muscular as Hercules, and with a countenance as open and as pleasant as one would wish to see. He was bought by General Alfred Bledser, and put on his River Place. He worked well for a few weeks, but got into trouble with the overseer, and finally compromised matters by taking to the woods. He seemed born for this particular business; for the track dogs failed to find him, and all the arts and artifices employed for capturing and reclaiming runaways failed in his case. It was a desperate sort of freedom he enjoyed; but he seemed suited to it, and he made the most of it.

As might be supposed, there was great commotion in the settlement, and particularly at the Kendrick homestead, when it was known that Blue Dave had been hiding among the gables of the Kendrick house. Mrs. Kendrick and her daughter Kitty possessed their full share of what Brother Roach would have called " spunk ; " but there is a large and very important corner of the human mind — particularly if it happens to be a feminine mind — which devotes itself to superstition; and these gentle ladies, while they stood in no terror of Blue Dave as a runaway negro simply, were certainly awed by the spectral figure which had grown up out of common report. The house negroes stood in mortal dread of Blue Dave, and their dismay was not without its effect upon Mrs. Kendrick and her daughter. Jenny, the house-girl, re-

fused to sleep at the quarters; and when Aunt
Tabby, the cook, started for her cabin after dark,
she was accompanied by a number of little negroes bearing lightwood torches. All the stories and legends that clustered around Blue
Dave's career were brought to the surface
again; and, as we have seen, the great majority
of them were anything but reassuring.

II.

WHILE the commotion in the settlement and
on the Kendrick Place was at its height, an incident occurred that had a tendency to relieve
Kitty Kendrick's mind. Shortly after the funeral the spring rains had set in, and for several days great floods came down from the skies.
One evening shortly after dark, Kitty Kendrick
stepped out upon the veranda, in an aimless
sort of way, to look at the clouds. The rain
had ceased, but the warm earth was reeking
with moisture. The trees and the ground were
smoking with fog, and great banks of vapor
were whirling across the sky from the south-
west. Kitty sighed. After a while George Denham would go rattling by in his buggy from
his law office in Rockville to his plantation, and
it was too dark to catch a glimpse of him. At

any rate, she would do the best she could. She would put the curtains of the sitting-room back, so the light could shine out, and perhaps George would stop to warm his hands and say a word to her mother. Kitty turned to go in when she heard her name called, —

"Miss Kitty!"

"Well, what is it?" Kitty was startled a little in spite of herself.

"Please, ma'am, don't be skeer'd."

"Why should I be frightened? What do you want?"

"Miss Kitty, I des come by fer ter tell you dat Murder Creek done come way out er its banks, en ef Mars. George Denham come by w'en he gwine on home, I wish you please, ma'am, be so good ez ter tell 'im dat dey ain't no fordin' place fer ter be foun' dar dis night."

The voice was that of a negro, and there was something in the tone of it that arrested Kitty Kendrick's attention.

"Who sent you?" she asked.

"Nobody ain't sont me; I des come by my-se'f. I laid off fer ter tell Mars. George, but I year talk he mighty headstrong, en I speck he des laugh at me."

"Are you one of our hands?"

"No, 'm; I don't b'long on de Kendrick Place."

"Come out of the shadow there where I can see you."

"I mos' fear'd, Miss Kitty."

"What is your name?"

"Dey calls me Blue Dave, ma'am."

The tone of the voice was something more than humble. There was an appeal in it for mercy. Kitty Kendrick recognized this; but in spite of it she could scarcely resist an impulse to rush into the house, lock the door, and take steps to rouse the whole plantation. By a great effort she did resist it, and the negro went on:—

"Please, ma'am, don't be skeer'd er me, Miss Kitty. De Lord years me w'en I say it, dey ain't a ha'r er yo' head dat I'd hurt, dat dey

ain't. I ain't bad like dey make out I is, Miss
Kitty. Dey tells some mighty big tales, but
dey makes um up dey se'f. Manys en manys
de time is I seed you w'en you gwine atter
sweet-gum en w'en you huntin' flowers, en I
allers say ter myse'f, I did, 'Nobody better not
pester Miss Kitty w'iles Blue Dave anywhars
'roun'.' Miss Kitty, I 'clar' 'fo' de Lord I
ain't no bad nigger," Blue Dave continued in
a tone of the most emphatic entreaty. "You
des ax yo' little br'er. Little Mars. Felix, he
knows I ain't no bad nigger."

"Why don't you go home, instead of hiding
out in the woods?" said Kitty, striving to speak
in a properly indignant tone.

"Bless yo' soul, Miss Kitty, hit ain't no
home fer me," said Blue Dave, sadly. "Hit
mought be a home fer some niggers, but hit
ain't no home fer me. I year somebody comin'.
Good-by, Miss Kitty; don't fergit 'bout Mars.
George."

As noiselessly as the wind that faintly stirs
the grass, Blue Dave glided away in the dark-

ness, leaving Kitty Kendrick standing upon the veranda half frightened and wholly puzzled. Her little brother Felix came out to see where she had gone. Felix was eight years old, and had views of his own.

"Sister Kit, what are you doing? Watching for Mr. George to go by?"

"Don't speak to me, you naughty boy!" exclaimed Kitty. "You've disgraced us all. You knew Blue Dave was hiding on top of the house all the while. What would be done with us if people found out we had been harboring a runaway negro?" Kitty pretended to be terribly shocked. Felix gave a long whistle, indicative of astonishment.

"You are awful smart," he said. "How did you find that out? Yes, I did know it," he went on desperately, "and I don't care if I did. If you tell anybody, I'll never run up the road to see if Mr. George is coming as long as I live; I won't never do anything for you."

Kitty's inference was based on what Blue Dave had said; but it filled her with dismay to find it true. She caught the child by the shoulder and gave him a little shake.

"Brother Felix, how dare you do such a thing? If mother knew of it, it would break her heart."

"Well, go and tell her and break her heart," said the boy, sullenly. "It was n't my fault that Blue Dave was up there. I did n't tote him up, I reckon."

"Oh, how could you do such a thing?" reiterated Kitty, putting her handkerchief to her eyes, as if by this means to expiate her brother's folly.

"Well," said the child, still speaking sullenly, "I heard something moving on top of the house one day when I was in the garret, and I kept on hearing it until I opened the window and went out on the roof. Then, when I got out there, I saw a great big nigger man."

"Were n't you frightened?" exclaimed Kitty, catching her breath. "What did you say?"

"I said 'Hello!' and then he jumped like he

was shot. I asked him his name, and he said
he was named Blue Dave, and he begged me so
hard I promised not to tell he was up there.
And then, after that, he used to come in the
garret and tell me no end of tales, and I've got
a trunk full of chestnuts that he brought me.
He's the best nigger man I ever saw, less'n
it's old Uncle Manuel, and he'll be as good as
Uncle Manuel when he gets that old, 'cause
Uncle Manuel said so. And I know it ain't
my fault; and if you want to tell mother you
can come and tell her right now, and then
you won't never be my sister any more, never,
never!"

"I think you have acted shamefully," said
Kitty. "Suppose he had come in the garret,
and made his way downstairs, and murdered us
all while we were asleep."

"Well," said Felix, "he could have come any
time. I wouldn't be afraid to go out in the
woods and stay with Blue Dave this very night,
and if I had my way he wouldn't be running from old Bill Brand and his dogs. When

I get a man I'm going to save up money
and buy Blue Dave. I thought at first I
wanted a pony, but I wouldn't have a pony
now."

While they were talking, Kitty heard the rattle of buggy wheels. The sound came nearer
and nearer. Whoever was driving was singing
to pass the time away, and the quick ear of
Kitty recognized the voice of George Denham.
He went dashing by; but he must have seen the
girl standing on the veranda, for he cried
out, "Good-night, Miss Kitty!" and then caught
up the burden of his song again as he went
whirling down the road. Kitty wrung her
hands. She went in to her mother with tears
in her eyes.

"Oh, mother! George has gone by without
stopping. What shall we do?"

Mrs. Kendrick was a very practical woman.
Knowing nothing of the freshet in Murder
Creek, she was amazed as well as amused at
Kitty's tragic attitude.

"Well, it's most too soon for George to be-

gin to take his meals here, I reckon," she said
dryly. "You'd better make you a cup of ginger-
tea and go to bed."

"But, mother, there's a freshet in Murder
Creek. Oh, why didn't he stop?"

Mrs. Kendrick was kneeling on the floor cut-
ting out clothes for the plough-hands, — "slav-
ing for her niggers," as she called it. She
paused in her work and looked at Kitty, as if
to see whether she had heard her aright.

"Well, upon my word!" she exclaimed, after
critically surveying her daughter, "I don't see
how girls can be so weak-minded. Many a
man as good as George Denham has crossed
Murder Creek in a freshet. I don't see but
what he's big enough and ugly enough to take
care of himself."

"Oh," exclaimed Kitty, going from window
to window, and vainly endeavoring to peer out
into the darkness, "why didn't he stop?"

"Well," said Mrs. Kendrick, resuming the
use of her shears, "if you'll try to worry along
and stand it this time, I'll send out and have

a fence built across the big road, and get the niggers to light a bonfire; and we'll stop him the next time he comes along. I'll have to do my duty by my own children, I reckon. But don't be alarmed," she continued, perceiving that Kitty's distress was genuine. "You may have to fly around here and get George some supper, after all. I've been waiting on niggers all day; and even if I had n't, I'm too old and fagged out to be rushing in amongst the pots and kettles to please George Denham."

George Denham rattled down the road, singing of "Barbara Allen," but thinking of Kitty Kendrick. Suddenly his horse shied, and then he heard somebody call him.

"Mars. George! Is dat you, Mars. George?"

"Unless you want to make a ghost of me by frightening my horse," exclaimed the young man, checking the animal with some difficulty. "What do you want?"

"Mars. George, is you see Miss Kitty w'en you come by des now?"

"No, I did n't stop. Is anything the matter?"

" No, sir, nothin' in 'tickler ain't de matter, 'ceppin' dat Miss Kitty had sump'n' ter tell you."

" Are you one of the Kendrick negroes ? "

" No, sir ; I don't b'long dar."

" Who are you ? "

" I 'clar' ter goodness, I skeer'd ter tell you, Mars. George ; kaze you mought fly up en git mad."

The young man laughed with such genuine heartiness that it did the negro good to hear it.

" Well, I know who you are," he said ; " you are Blue Dave, and you 've come to tell me that you want me to carry you to jail, where Bill Brand can get his hands on you."

The negro was thunderstruck. " 'Fo' de Lord, Mars. George ! how you know who I is ? "

" Why, I know by your looks. You 've got horns and a club foot. That 's the way the Old Boy fixes himself."

" Now, Mars. George," said the negro, in a grieved tone, " ef you could see me good you would n't set dar en say I 'm a bad-lookin' nigger."

"Are you really Blue Dave?" the young man asked, dropping his bantering tone and speaking seriously.

"Yasser, Mars. George; I'm dat ve'y nigger."

"What do you want with me?"

"I des wanter tell you, Mars. George, dat dey's a freshet come fum 'bove, en Murder Creek is 'way out'n hits banks. You can't cross dar wid no hoss en buggy dis night."

The young man reflected a moment. He was more interested in the attitude of the negro than he was in the extent of the freshet or the danger of an attempt to cross the creek.

"I've a knack of crossing Murder Creek in a freshet," he said. "But why should you want to keep me out of it?"

"Well, sir, fer one thing," said Blue Dave, shifting about on his feet uneasily, "you look so much like my young marster w'at died in Ferginny. En den dat day w'en de speckerlater put me up on de block, you 'uz settin' dar straddle er yo' pony, en you 'lowed dat he oughter

be 'shame er hisse'f fer ter chain me up dat
a-way."

"Oh, I remember. I made quite a fool of
myself that day."

"Yasser; en den w'en de man say sump'n'
sassy back, little ez you wuz, you spurred de
pony at 'im en tole 'im you 'd slap 'im in de jaw.
He 'uz de skeer'dest w'ite man I ever see. I
say ter myse'f den dat I hope de day 'd come
w'en dat little boy 'd grow up en buy me; en
dat make I say w'at I does. I want you to keep
out 'n dat creek dis night, en den I want you
ter buy me. Please, sir, buy me, Mars. George;
I make you de bes' nigger you ever had."

"Why, great Jerusalem! you would n't be on
my place a week before you 'd get your feelings
hurt and rush off to the woods, and I 'd never
see you any more."

"Des try me, Mars. George! des try me. I 'll
work my arms off ter de elbows, en den I 'll
work wid de stumps. Des try me, Mars.
George!"

"I expect you would be a right good hand if

you hadn't been free so long. Go home and let me see how you can work for your master, and then maybe I'll think about buying you."

"Eh-eh, Mars. George! I better go jump in a burnin' bresh-pile. Ain't you gwine ter tu'n back, Mars. George?"

"Not to-night. Go home and behave yourself."

With that George Denham clucked to his restive horse, and went clattering down the road in the direction of Murder Creek, which crossed the highway a mile farther on. Blue Dave stood still a moment, scratching his head and looking after the buggy.

"Is anybody ever see de beat er dat?" he exclaimed. "Ef Mars. George gits in dat creek dey's got ter be a merakel come 'bout ef he gits out." He stood in the road a moment longer, still scratching his head as if puzzled. Then he addressed himself indignantly. "Looky yer, nigger, w'at you stan'in' yer fer? Whar yo' manners, whar yo' perliteness?"

Thus, half-humorously, half-seriously, talking

to himself, Blue Dave went trotting along in the direction taken by George Denham. He moved without apparent exertion, but with amazing swiftness. But the young man in the buggy had also moved swiftly; and, go as fast as he might, Blue Dave could not hope to overtake him before he reached the creek.

For George Denham was impatient to get home, — as impatient as his horse, which did not need even the lightest touch of the whip to urge it forward. He paid no attention to the familiar road. He was thinking of pretty Kitty Kendrick, and of the day, not very far in the future he hoped, when, in going home, he should be driving towards her instead of away from her. He paid no attention to the fact that, as he neared the creek, his horse subsided from a swinging trot to a mincing gait that betrayed indecision; nor did it strike him as anything unusual that the horse should begin to splash water with his feet long before he had reached the banks of the creek; no doubt it was a pool left standing in the road after the heavy rains.

But the pool steadily grew deeper; and while George Denham was picturing Kitty Kendrick sitting on one side of his fireplace and his old mother on the other, — his old mother, with her proud face and her stately ways, — his horse stopped and looked around. Young Denham slapped the animal with the reins, without taking note of his surroundings. Thus reassured, the horse went on; but the water grew deeper and deeper, and presently the creature stopped again. This time it smelt of the water and emitted the low, deeply drawn snort by which horses betray their uneasiness; and when George Denham would have urged it forward, it struck the water impatiently with its forefoot. Aroused by this, the young man looked around; but there was nothing to warn him of his danger. The fence that would otherwise have been a landmark, was gone. There was no loud and angry roaring of the floods. Behind him the shifting clouds, the shining stars, and the blue patches of sky mirrored themselves duskily and vaguely in the slow creeping waters; before

him the shadows of the trees that clustered
somewhere near the banks of the creek were so
deep and heavy that they seemed to merge the
dark waters of the flood into the gloom of the
night. When the horse was quiet, peering ahead,
with its sharp little ears pointed forward, there
was no sound save the vague sighing of the
wind through the tops of the scrub pines and
the gentle ripple of the waters.

As George Denham urged his horse forward,
confident of his familiarity with the surroundings, Blue Dave ran up on the little ridge to
the left through which the road had been cut
or worn.

"Mars. George!" he shouted, "don't you see
wharbouts you is! Wait, Mars. George! Pull
dat hoss up!"

But Blue Dave was too late. As he spoke,
the horse and buggy plunged into the flood, and
for a moment they were lost to view. Then
the struggling animal seemed to strike rising
ground; but the buggy was caught in the re-
sistless current, and, with George Denham

14

clinging to it, it dragged the horse down, and the swirling waters seemed to sweep over and beyond them. Blue Dave lost not a moment. Flinging himself into the flood from the vantage ground on which he stood, a few strokes of his sinewy arms carried him to where he saw George Denham disappear. That young man was an expert swimmer; and though the sudden immersion had taken him at a disadvantage, he would have made his way out with little difficulty but for the fact that a heavy piece of driftwood had been hurled against his head. Stunned, but still conscious, he was making an ineffectual attempt to reach the shore when he was caught by Blue Dave and borne safely back to land. The horse, in its struggles, had succeeded in tearing itself loose from the buggy, and they heard it crawl up the bank on the other side and shake itself. Blue Dave carried George Denham out of the water as one would carry a child. When he had set the young man down in a comparatively dry place, he exclaimed with a grin, —

"Dar now, Mars. George! w'at I tell you? Little mo' en de tarrypins would 'a' bin a-nibblin' atter you."

George Denham was dazed as well as weak. He put his hand to his head and tried to laugh.

"You were just in time, old fellow," he said.

Then he got on his feet and tried to walk, but he would have sunk down again but for Blue Dave's arm.

"Why, I'm as weak as a stray cat," he exclaimed feebly. "Let me lie down here a moment."

"Dat I won't, Mars. George! dat I won't! I tuck 'n' brung you out, en now I'm a-gwineter take 'n' ca'er you back dar whar Miss Kitty waitin'."

"Well, you'll have to wait until I can walk."

"No, sir; I'll des squat down, en you kin crawl up on my back des like you useter play hoss."

"Why, you can't carry me, old fellow; I'm too heavy for that."

"Shoo! don't you b'leeve de half er dat, Mars.

George. I toted bigger turns dan w'at you is long 'fo' I had de strenk w'at I got now. Grab me 'roun' de neck, Mars. George; git up little higher. Now, den, don't you be fear'd er fallin'."

Blue Dave rose from his stooping posture, steadied himself a moment, and then moved on with his living burden. He moved slowly and cautiously at first, but gradually increased his pace to a swinging walk that carried him forward with surprising swiftness.

To George Denham it all seemed like a dream. He suffered no pain, and it was with a sort of queer elation of mind that he felt the huge muscles of the negro swell and subside under him with the regularity of machinery, and knew that every movement carried him toward Kitty Kendrick and — rest. He was strangely tired, but not otherwise uncomfortable. He felt abundantly grateful to this poor runaway negro, and thought that if he could overcome his mother's prejudices (she had a horror of runaway negroes) he would buy Blue Dave and make him

comfortable. Thus they swung along until the
negro's swift stride brought them to Mrs. Kendrick's gate. There Blue Dave deposited George
Denham, and exclaimed with a laugh as he
leaned against the fence, —

"You 'er right smart chunk er meat, Mars.
George, ez sho ez de worl'!"

George Denham also leaned against the fence,
but he did n't laugh. He was thinking of what
seemed to him a very serious matter.

"Mother will be frightened to death when
that horse gets home," he said.

"You go in dar en get wom, Mars. George,"
said Blue Dave. "I 'm gwine 'roun' by de High
Bridge en tell um whar you is."

"Why, you'll break yourself down," said
George Denham.

"Ah, Lord, Mars. George!" said the negro,
laughing, "time you bin in de woods long ez I
is de four mile 'twix' yer en yo' house 'll look
mighty short. Go in dar, Mars. George, 'fo'
you git col'!"

Shortly after this, George Denham was in bed

and fast asleep. He had been met at the door by Kitty Kendrick, in whose tell-tale face the blushes of that heartiest of all welcomes had chased away the pallor of dread and anxiety. Mrs. Kendrick was less sympathetic in word than in deed. She had known George Denham since he was a little boy in short clothes; and while she approved of him, and had a sort of motherly affection for him, she was disposed to be critical, as are most women who have the knack of management.

"And so you've come back dripping, have you? Well, you ain't the first headstrong, high-strung chap that's found out water is wet when the creek blots out the big road, I reckon. I'm no duck myself. When I see water, I'm like the old cat in the corner; I always feel like shaking my foot. Kitty, call Bob and tell him to make a fire in the big room. He's asleep, I reckon, and you'll have to holler. Set a nigger down and he's snoring directly. You look pale," Mrs. Kendrick continued, turning to George. "You must have gone in over your ears. I should think a drenching like that would take all the conceit out of a man."

"Well, it has taken it all out of me, ma'am," said George, laughing. Then the young man told Mrs. Kendrick of his misadventure, and of the part Blue Dave had borne in it.

"He's the nigger that roosted on top of my house," said Mrs. Felix, bustling around and putting a kettle of water on the fire. "Well, it's a roundabout way to pay for his lodging, but it's the best he could do, I reckon. Now, don't you worry yourself, George; in ten minutes you'll be snug in bed, and then you'll drink a cup of composition tea, and to-morrow morning you'll have forgotten all about trying to make a spring branch out of Murder Creek."

As the successful mistress of a household, Mrs. Kendrick knew precisely what was necessary to be done. There was no hitch in her system, no delay in her methods, and no disputing her remedies. George Denham was ordered to bed as if he had been a child; and though the "composition" tea was hot in the mouth and bitter to the palate, it was useless to protest against it. As a consequence of all this, the young man was soon in the land of dreams.

When everything was quiet, Kitty prepared a very substantial lunch. Then, calling her little brother Felix, she went across the yard to the quarters, and stopped at Uncle Manuel's cabin. The door was ajar, and Kitty could see the venerable old negro nodding before the flickering embers. She went in and called his name, —

"Uncle Manuel!"

"Eh! Who dat?" Then, looking around and perceiving Kitty, the old negro's weather-beaten face shone with a broad smile of surprise and welcome. "Why, honey! Why, little Mistiss! How come dis? You makes de ole nigger feel proud; dat you does. I fear'd ter ax you ter set down, honey, de cheer so rickety."

"Uncle Manuel," said Kitty, "do you know Blue Dave?"

Uncle Manuel was old, and wise, and cunning. He hesitated a moment before replying;

and even then his caution would not allow him to commit himself.

"Blue Dave, he's dat ar runaway nigger, ain't he, honey? I done year talk un 'im lots er times."

"Well," said Kitty, placing her basket upon Uncle Manuel's tool-chest, "here is something for Blue Dave to eat. If you don't see him yourself, perhaps you can send it to him by some one."

Uncle Manuel picked up the basket, weighed it in his hand, and then placed it on the chest again. Then he looked curiously at Kitty, and said, —

"Honey, how come you gwine do dis? Ain't you year tell hit's ag'in de law fer ter feed a runaway nigger?"

Kitty blushed as she thought of George Denham. "I send Blue Dave the victuals because I choose to, Uncle Manuel," she said. "The law has nothing to do with that little basket."

She started to go, but Uncle Manuel raised both hands heavenwards.

" Wait, little Mistiss," he cried, the tears running down his furrowed face; " des wait, little Mistiss. 'T won't hurt you, honey. De ole nigger wuz des gwine ter git down ter his pra'rs 'fo' you come in. Dey ain't no riper time dan dis."

Uncle Manuel's voice was husky with suppressed emotion. With his hands still stretched toward the skies, and the tears still running down his face, he fell upon his knees and exclaimed, —

" Saviour en Marster er de worl'! draw nigh dis night en look down into dis ole nigger's heart; lissen ter de humblest er de humble. Blessed Marster! some run wild en some go stray, some go hether en some go yan'; but all un um mus' go befo' dy mercy-seat in de een'. Some'll fetch big works en some'll fetch great deeds, but po' ole Manuel won't fetch nothin' but one weak, sinful heart. Dear, blessed Marster! look in dat heart en see w'at in dar. De sin dat's dar, Lord, blot it out wid dy wounded han'. Dear Marster, bless my little Mistiss.

Her comin's en her gwines is des like one er dy angels er mercy; she scatters bread en meat 'mongs' dem w'at's lonesome in der ways, en dem w'at runs up en down in de middle er big tribalation. Saviour! Marster! look down 'pon my little Mistiss; gedder her 'nead dy hev'mly wings. Ef trouble mus' come, let it come 'pon me. I'm ole, but I'm tough; I'm ole, but I got de strenk. Lord! let de troubles en de trials come 'pon de ole nigger w'at kin stan' um, en save my little Mistiss fum sheddin' one tear. En den, at de las' fetch us all home ter hev'm, whar dey's res' fer de w'ary. Amen."

Never in her life before had Kitty felt so thrilling a sense of nearness to her Creator as when Uncle Manuel was offering up his simple prayer; and she went out of the humble cabin weeping gently.

III.

THE four-mile run to the Denham Plantation was fun for Blue Dave. He was wet and cold, and the exercise acted as a lively invigorant. Once, as he sped along, he was challenged by the patrol; but he disappeared like a shadow, and came into the road again a mile away, singing to himself, —

> Run, nigger, run! patter-roller ketch you;
> Run, nigger, run! hit's almos' day!

He was well acquainted with the surroundings at the Denham Plantation, having been fed many a time by the well-cared-for negroes; and he had no hesitation in approaching the premises. The clouds had whirled themselves away, and the stars told him it was ten o'clock. There was a light in the sitting-room, and Blue Dave judged it best to go to the back door. He rapped gently, and then a little louder. Ordinarily the door would have been opened by the trim black housemaid; but to-night it was opened by George Denham's mother, a prim old lady of whom everybody stood greatly in awe without precisely knowing why. She looked out, and saw the gigantic negro looming up on the doorsteps.

"Do you bring news of my son?" she asked. The voice was low, but penetrating; and the calm, even tones told the story of a will too strong to tolerate opposition or even contradiction.

Blue Dave hesitated out of sheer embarrassment at finding such cool serenity where he had probably expected to find grief or some such excitement.

"Did you hear me speak?" the prim old lady asked, before the negro had time to gather his wits. "Do you bring me news of my son?"

"Yessum," said Blue Dave, scratching his head; "dat w'at I come fer. Mars. George gwine ter stay at de Kendrick Place ter-night.

I speck he in bed by dis time," he added reassuringly.

"His horse has come home without buggy or harness. Is my son hurt? Don't be afraid to tell me the truth. What has happened to him?"

How could the poor negro — how could anybody — know what a whirlwind of yearning affection, dread, and anxiety was raging behind these cool, level tones?

"Mistiss, I tell you de trufe: Mars. George is sorter hurted, but he ain't hurted much. I met 'im in de road, en I tuck 'n' tole 'im dey wuz a freshet in Murder Creek; but he des laugh at me, en he driv' in des like dey wa'n't no water dar; en den w'en he make his disappearance, I tuck 'n' splunge in atter 'im, en none too soon, n'er, kaze he got strucken on de head wid a log, en w'en I fotch 'im out, he 'uz all dazzle up like. Yit he ain't hurted much, Mistiss."

"What is your name?" the prim old lady asked.

"Blue Dave, ma'am."

" The runaway ? "

The negro hesitated, looked around, and then hung down his head. He knew the calm, fearless eyes of this gentlewoman were upon him; he felt the influence of her firm tones. She repeated her question: —

" Are you Blue Dave, the runaway ? "

" Yessum."

The answer seemed to satisfy the lady. She turned and called Eliza, the housemaid.

" Eliza, your master's supper is in the dining-room by the fire. Here are the keys. Take it into the kitchen." Then she turned to Blue Dave. " David," she said, " go into the kitchen and eat your supper."

Then Eliza was sent after Ellick, the negro foreman; and Ellick was not long in finding Blue Dave a suit of linsey-woolsey clothes, a little warmer and a little drier than those the runaway was in the habit of wearing. Then the big grays were put to the Denham carriage, shawls and blankets were thrown in, and Blue Dave was called.

"Have you had your supper, David?" said Mrs. Denham, looking grimmer than ever as she stood on her veranda arrayed in bonnet and wraps.

"Thanky, Mistiss! thanky, ma'am. I ain't had no meal's vittles like dat, not sence I lef' Ferginny."

"Can you drive a carriage, David?" the old lady asked.

"Dat I kin, Mistiss."

Whereupon he seized the reins and let down the carriage steps. Mrs. Denham and her maid got in; but when everything was ready, Blue Dave hesitated.

"Mistiss," he said, rather sheepishly, "w'en I come 'long des now, de patter-rollers holler'd atter me."

"No matter, David," the grim old lady replied; "your own master would n't order you off of *my* carriage."

"Keep yo' eye on dat off hoss!" exclaimed Ellick, as the carriage moved off.

"Hush, honey," Blue Dave cried, as exult-

antly as a child; "'fo' dey gits ter de big gate,
I'll know deze yer hosses better dan ef dey
wuz my br'er."

After that, nothing more was said. The road
had been made firm and smooth by the heavy
beating rain, and the carriage swung along
easily and rapidly. The negro housemaid fell
back against the cushions, and was soon sound
asleep; but Mrs. Denham sat bolt-upright.
Hers was an uncompromising nature, it had
been said, and certainly it seemed so; but as
the carriage rolled along, there grew before her
mind's eye the vague, dim outlines of a vision,—
a vision of a human creature hiding in the dark
swamps, fleeing through the deep woods and
creeping swiftly through the pine thickets. It
was a pathetic figure, this fleeing human creature, whether chased by dogs and men or pursued only by the terrors that hide themselves
behind the vast shadows of the night; and the
figure grew more pathetic when, as it seemed,
it sprang out of the very elements themselves
to snatch her son from the floods. The old

15

lady sighed and pressed her thin lips together.
She had made up her mind.

Presently the carriage drew up at the Kendrick Place; and in a little while, after effusive
greetings all around, Mrs. Denham was sitting
at Mrs. Kendrick's hearth listening to the story
of her son's rescue. She wanted to go in and
see George at once, but Mrs. Kendrick would
consent only on condition that he was not to
be aroused.

"It is foolish to say it," said the old lady,
smiling at Kitty as she came out of the room in
which her son was sleeping; "but my son seems
to look to-night just as he did when a baby."

Kitty smiled such a responsive smile, and
looked so young and beautiful, that the proud
old lady stooped and kissed her.

"I think I shall love you, my dear."

"I reckon I'll have to get even with you,"
said Mrs. Kendrick, who had a knack of hiding
her own emotion, "by telling George that I've
fallen in love with him."

This gave a light and half-humorous turn to affairs, and in a moment Mrs. Denham was as prim and as uncompromising in appearance as ever.

"Well!" exclaimed Mrs. Kendrick, after she and Kitty had retired for the night, "the day's worth living if only to find out that Rebecca Denham has got a heart in her insides. I believe actually she'd 'a' cried for a little."

"She did cry, mother," said Kitty, solemnly. "There were tears in her eyes when she leaned over me."

"Well, well, well!" said Mrs. Kendrick, "she always put me in mind of a ghost that can't be laid on account of its pride. But we're what the Lord made us, I reckon, and people deceive their looks. My old turkey gobbler is harmless as a hound puppy; but I reckon he'd bust if he did n't up and strut when strangers are in the front porch."

With that Mrs. Kendrick addressed herself to her prayers and to slumber; but Kitty lay awake a long time, thinking and thinking, until finally her thoughts became the substance of youth's sweetest dreams.

IV.

But why should the tender dreams of this pure heart be transcribed here? Indeed, why should these vague outlines be spun out to the vanishing point, like the gossamer threads that float and glance and disappear in the September skies? Some of the grandchildren of George Denham and Kitty Kendrick will read these pages, and wonder, romantic youngsters that they are, why all the love passages have been suppressed; other readers, more practical and perhaps severer, will ask themselves what possible interest there can be in the narrative of a simple episode in the life of a humble fugitive. What reply can be made, what explanation can be offered? Fortunately, what remains to be told may mostly be put in the sententious language of Brother Johnny Roach.

One day, shortly after the events which have been described, Brother Brannum rode up to Brother Roach's mill, dismounted, and hitched his horse to the rack.

" You're mighty welcome, Brother Brannum," said Brother Roach from the door, as cheerful under his covering of meal dust as the clown in the pantomime; "you're mighty welcome. I had as lief talk to my hopper as to most folks; but the hopper knows me by heart, and I dassent take too many liberties wi' it. Come in, Brother Brannum; there's no great head of water on, and the gear is running soberly. Sat'days, when all the rocks are moving, my mill is a female woman; the clatter is turrible. I'll not deny it. I hope you're well, Brother Brannum. And Sister Brannum. I'll never forgit the savor of her Sunday dumplings, not if I live a thousand year."

" We're well as common, Brother Roach, well as common. Yit a twitch here and a twinge there tells us we're moving along to'rds eternity. It's age that's a-feeling of us, Brother Roach; and when we're ripe it'll pluck us."

" It's age ruther than the dumplings, that I'll take the stand on," exclaimed Brother Roach. " Yit, when it comes to that, look at Mizzers Denham; that woman kin look age out of countenance any day. Then there's Giner'l Bledser; who more nimble at a muster than the Gener'l? I see 'em both this last gone Sat'day, and though I was in-about up to my eyes in the toll-bin, I relished the seeing and the hearing of 'em. But I reckon you've heard the news, Brother Brannum," said Brother Roach, modestly deprecating his own sources of information.

" Bless you! Not me, Brother Roach," said Brother Brannum; "I've heard no news. Down in my settlement I'm cut off from the world. Let them caper as they may, we're not pestered wi' misinformation."

" No, nor me nuther, Brother Brannum," said Brother Roach, " bekaze it's as much as I can do for to listen at the racket of my mill. Yit there are some sights meal dust won't begin to hide, and some talk the clatter of the hopper won't nigh drown."

"What might they be, Brother Roach?" Brother Brannum brushed the dust off a box with his coat-tails, and sat down.

"Well, sir," said Brother Roach, pushing his hat back, and placing his thumbs behind his suspenders, "last Sat'day gone I was a-hurrying to and fro, when who should pop in at the door but Giner'l Bledser?

"'Hello, Johnny!' says he, free and familiar.

"'Howdy, Giner'l,' says I. 'You look holp up, speaking off-hand,' says I.

"'That I am, Johnny, that I am,' says he; 'I've made a trade that makes me particular proud,' says he.

"'How's that, Giner'l?' says I.

"'Why, I've sold Blue Dave,' says he; 'eight year ago, I bought him for five hundred dollars, and now I've sold him to Mizzers Denham for a thousand,' says he. 'I've got the cold cash in my pocket, and now let 'em ketch the nigger,' says he.

"'Well, Giner'l,' says I, 'it'll be time for to marvel arter you see the outcome, bekaze,' says I, 'when there's business in the wind, Mizzers Denham is as long-headed and as cle'r-sighted as a Philadelphia lawyer,' says I.

"And (would you believe it, Brother Brannum?) the outcome happened then and there right before our very face and eyes."

"In what regards, Brother Roach?" said Brother Brannum, rubbing his bony hands together.

"Well, sir, I glanced my eye out of the door, and I see the Denham carriage coming down yan hill. I p'inted it out to the Giner'l, and he ups and says, says he, —

"'Davy, though she may be a-going to town for to sue me for damages, yit, if Mizzers Denham's in that carriage, I'll salute her now,' says he; and then he took his stand in the door, as frisky as a colt and as smiling as a basket of chips. As they come up, I tetch'd the Giner'l on the shoulder.

"'Giner'l,' says I, 'look clost at that nig-

ger on the carriage,—look clost at him,'
says I.

" ' Why, what the thunderation ! ' says he.

" 'To be certain ! ' says I; 'that's your Blue
Dave, and he looks mighty slick,' says I.

" The Giner'l forgot for to say howdy," continued Brother Roach, laughing until he began
to wheeze; " but Mizzers Denham, she leant out
of the carriage window, and said, says she, —

" ' Good-morning, Giner'l, good-morning !
David is a most excellent driver,' says she.

"The Giner'l managed for to take off his
hat, but he was in-about the worst whipped-out
white man I ever see. And arter the carriage
got out of hearing, sir, he stood in that there
door there and cussed plump tell he couldn't
cuss. When a man's been to Congress and
back, he's liable for to know how to take the
name of the Lord in vain. But don't tell me
about the wimmen, Brother Brannum. Don't ! "

Blue Dave was happy at last. He became a
great favorite with everybody. His voice was

the loudest at the corn-shucking, his foot was the nimblest at the plantation frolics, his row was the straightest and the cleanest in the cotton-patch, his hand was the firmest on the carriage-seat, his arm was the strongest at the log-rolling. When his old mistress came to die, her wandering mind dwelt upon the negro who had served her so faithfully. She fancied she was making a journey.

"The carriage goes smoothly along here," she said. Then, after a little pause she asked, "Is David driving?" and the weeping negro cried out from a corner of the room, —

"'T ain't po' Dave, Mistiss! De good Lord done tuck holt er de lines."

And so, dreaming as a little child would dream, the old lady slipped from life into the beatitudes, if the smiles of the dead mean anything.

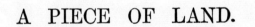

A PIECE OF LAND.

A PIECE OF LAND.

THE history of Pinetucky District in Putnam County is preserved in tradition only, but its records are not less savory on that account. The settlement has dispersed and disappeared, and the site of it is owned and occupied by a busy little man, who wears eyeglasses and a bob-tailed coat, and who is breeding Jersey cattle and experimenting with ensilage. It is well for this little man's peace of mind that the dispersion was an accomplished fact before he made his appearance. The Jersey cattle would have been winked at, and the silo regarded as an object of curiosity; but the eyeglasses and the bob-tailed coat would not have been tolerated. But if Pinetucky had its peculiarities, it also had its advantages. It was pleased with

its situation and surroundings, and was not puzzled, as a great many people have since been,
as to the origin of its name. In brief, Pinetucky was satisfied with itself. It was a
sparsely settled neighborhood, to be sure, but
the people were sociable and comparatively
comfortable. They could remain at home, so
to speak, and attend the militia musters, and
they were in easy reach of a church-building
which was not only used by all denominations —
Methodists, Baptists, and Presbyterians — as a
house of worship, but was made to serve as a
schoolhouse. So far as petty litigation was
concerned, Squire Ichabod Inchly, the wheel-
wright, was prepared to hold justice-court in the
open air in front of his shop when the weather
was fine, and in any convenient place when the
weather was foul. " Gentlemen," he would say,
when a case came before him, " I'd a heap
ruther shoe a horse or shrink a tire; yit if you
will have the law, I'll try and temper it wi' jes-
tice." This was the genuine Pinetucky spirit,
and all true Pinetuckians tried to live up to it.

When occasion warranted they followed the example of larger communities and gossiped about each other; but rural gossip is oftener harmless than not; besides, it is a question whether gossip does not serve a definite moral purpose. If our actions are to be taken note of by people whose good opinion is worth striving for, the fact serves as a motive and a cue for orderly behavior.

Yet it should be said that the man least respected by the Pinetuckians was the man least gossiped about. This was Bradley Gaither, the richest man in the neighborhood. With few exceptions, all the Pinetuckians owned land and negroes; but Bradley Gaither owned more land and more negroes than the most of them put together. No man, to all appearances, led a more correct life than Bradley Gaither. He was first at church, and the last to leave; he even affected a sort of personal interest in politics; but the knack of addressing himself to the respect and esteem of his neighbors he lacked altogether. He was not parsimonious, but, as Squire Inchly expressed it, "narrer-minded in money-matters." He had the air of a man who is satisfied with himself rather than with the world, and the continual exhibition of this species of selfishness is apt to irritate the most simple-minded spectator. Lacking the sense of humor necessary to give him a knowledge of his own relations to his neighbors, he lived under the impression that he was not only one of the most generous of men, but the most popular. He insisted upon his rights. If people made bad bargains when they traded with him, — and he allowed them to make no other kind, — they must stand or fall by them. Where his lands joined those of his neighbors, there was always "a lane for the rabbits," as the saying is. He would join fences with none of them. Indeed, he was a surly neighbor, though he did not even suspect the fact.

He had one weakness, — a greed for land. If he drove hard bargains, it was for the purpose of adding to his landed possessions. He overworked and underfed his negroes in order

that he might buy more land. Day and night
he toiled, and planned, and pinched himself
and the people around him to gratify his land-
hunger.

Bradley Gaither had one redeeming feature,
—his daughter Rose. For the sake of this
daughter Pinetucky was willing to forgive him
a great many things. To say that Rose Gaither
was charming or lovely, and leave the matter
there, would ill become even the casual historian of Pinetucky. She was lovely, but her
loveliness was of the rare kind that shows itself in strength of character as well as in
beauty of form and feature. In the apprecia-
tive eyes of the Pinetuckians she seemed to
invest womanhood with a new nobility. She
possessed dignity without vanity, and her can-
dor was tempered by a rare sweetness that won
all hearts. She carried with her that mysterious flavor of romance that belongs to the
perfection of youth and beauty ; and there are
old men in Rockville to-day, sitting in the sunshine on the street corners and dreaming of

16

the past, whose eyes will kindle with enthusiasm
at mention of Rose Gaither's name.

But in 1840 Bradley Gaither's beautiful
daughter was not by any means the only representative of womankind in Pinetucky. There
was Miss Jane Inchly, to go no further. Miss
Jane was Squire Inchly's maiden sister; and
though she was neither fat nor fair, she was
forty. Perhaps she was more than forty; but
if she was fifty she was not ashamed of it.
She had a keen eye and a sharp tongue, and
used both with a freedom befitting her sex and
her experience.

Squire Inchly's house was convenient to his
shop; and just opposite lived the Carews, father
and son, once the most prosperous and prominent family in the neighborhood. It was the
custom of Pinetucky to take a half-holiday on
Saturdays, and on one of these occasions
Squire Inchly, instead of going to his shop or
to the store, sat in his porch and smoked his
pipe. After awhile Miss Jane brought out her
sewing and sat with him. Across the way,

Uncle Billy Carew sat in his easy-chair under the shade of a tree, and made queer gestures in the air with his hands and cane, while his son, a young man of twenty-five or thereabouts, paced moodily up and down the veranda. The birds fluttered in and out of the hedges of Cherokee rose that ran along both sides of the road, and over all the sun shone brightly.

"Billy is cuttin' up his antics ag'in," said the Squire, finally. "First the limbs give way, and then the mind. It's Providence, I reckon. We're all a-gittin' old."

"Why, you talk, Ichabod, as if Providence went around with a drink of dram in one hand and a stroke of palsy in t'other one," said Miss Jane. "It's the Old Boy that totes the dram. And don't you pester yourself on account of old Billy Carew's palsy. A man's nimble enough in the legs when he can git to the dimmy-john."

"Well, I'm sorry for Jack, Sister Jane," exclaimed the Squire, heartily. "I am, from the bottom of my heart. The boy is too lonesome in his ways. He needs comp'ny; he needs to be holp up, Sister Jane. He does, certain and shore."

"Well, we're all near-sighted; but when I'm in trouble, I'm like a hen a-layin'; I don't want nobody to stand around and watch me. Not even them that feeds me. The Lord knows what he keeps old Billy Carew here to fret poor Jack for, but I don't," continued Miss Jane, with a sigh. "I'm much mistaken if that old creetur hain't got years before him to drink and dribble in."

"It passes me, Sister Jane," said Squire Inchly, moving uneasily in his chair. "It passes me, certain and shore. Here was Billy, rich and healthy, Jack at college and ever'thing a-runnin' slick and smooth, when nothin' must do but the old creetur must take to the jug, and it's gone on and gone on, till old Bradley Gaither owns in-about all the Carew plantation that's wuth ownin'. Maybe it was Billy's wife driv him to it, Sister Jane."

"I say the word!" exclaimed Miss Jane,

scornfully, — "I say the word! How could a little bit of a dried-up 'oman drive a grown man to drink?"

"They are a heap livelier than they look to be, Sister Jane," said the Squire, reassuringly. "Little as she was, I lay Billy Carew's wife had her say."

"Well," said Miss Jane, "a mouse'll squeal if you tromple on it."

Squire Inchly had a jovial appearance ordinarily; but when he found it necessary to wrestle with the moral problems that the sharp tongue of his sister presented to his mind, he was in the habit of putting on his spectacles, as if by that means to examine them more impartially. He put his spectacles on now, and with them a severe judicial frown.

"That's the trouble, Sister Jane, — that's the trouble," he said after awhile. "The mouse'll squeal and squeal, but where's the man that ever got use to sech squealin'?"

"Don't pester the mouse then," said Miss Jane, sententiously.

" Old Bradley Gaither," remarked the Squire, showing a disposition to wander away from a dangerous discussion, — " Old Bradley Gaither ain't only got mighty nigh all the Carew plantation, but he 's hot arter the balance of it. Last sale-day, he took me off behind the Courthouse, and, says he, —

" ' Square,' says he, ' I 'd like mighty well for to git that Carew place,' says he.

" ' Why, Mr. Gaither,' says I, ' you 've inabout got it all now,' says I.

" ' Square Ichabod,' says he, ' it 's only a matter of two hundred acres or thereabouts, and it cuts right spang into my plantation,' says he.

" ' Well,' says I, ' two hundred acres hain't much, yit arter all it 's a piece of land,' says I.

" ' That 's so,' says he, ' but I want that land, and I 'm willin' for to pay reasonable. I want you to buy it for me, Square,' says he.

" Right across from where we sot," the Squire continued, taking off his spectacles, " old Billy Carew was a cuttin' up and singin' his

worldly-reminded songs, and Jack was a-tryin'
for to git him off home.

"'Mr. Gaither,' says I, 'do you want to
crowd that poor old creetur out'n the county?'
says I. 'And look at Jack; you won't find a
better-favored youngster,' says I.

"I disremember what he said," the Squire
went on; "but when I named Jack he puckered
up them thin lips of his'n like he was fortifyin'
his mind ag'in anger. I didn't let on about
Rose and Jack, Sister Jane, but I reckon Mr.
Gaither has got his suspicions. No doubt he
has got his suspicions, Sister Jane."

"Ichabod," said Miss Jane, scratching her
head with the long teeth of her tucking-comb,
"you're too old to be made a tool of. Let old
Bradley Gaither do his own buyin' and sellin'.
That old scamp is deep as a well. Them that
didn't know him'd think he was sanctified; yit
he's got devilment enough in him to break
the winders out'n the meetin'-house. Well,
he needn't pester wi' Jack and Rose," Miss
Jane went on; "Jack'll never marry Rose

whiles old Billy Carew is hoppin' along betwixt
the grocery and the graveyard. Lord, Lord!
to think that sech a no-'count old creetur as
that should be a-ha'ntin' the face of the
earth!"

"He took to fiddlin' and drinkin' arter he
was fifty year old," remarked the Squire.

"Yes, and the property he hain't drunk up,
he's fiddled away, till now he hain't got nothin'
but a passel of half-free niggers and a little
piece of land, and old Bradley Gaither is hongry for that. And that ain't all," exclaimed
Miss Jane, solemnly; "Jack is ruined, and Rose
is distracted."

"Ah!" said the Squire.

"Yes," said Miss Jane. "Trouble is always
double and thribble. Rose was here last Tuesday, and she sot by the winder there and
watched Jack all the time she stayed.

"'That's what I call courtship at long taw,'
s' I.

"'Yes, Miss Jane,' se' she, 'it is, and I'm in
a great deal of trouble about Jack. I under-

stand him, but he don't understand me,' se' she.
'He's mad because my father loaned his father
money and then took land to pay for it. But
I'd marry Jack,' se' she, 'if only to give him
his land back.'

"I declare!" Miss Jane continued, "'t would
'a' melted airy heart in the universe to see that
child blushin' an' cryin'. I went and stood by
her and put my arms round her, and I says to
her, s' I, —

"'Don't you fret, honey, don't you fret. Old
Billy Carew is full of capers and vain babblin's,'
s' I, 'and your pappy is puffed up by his fleshly
mind; but the Almighty, he's a-watchin' 'em.
He'll fetch 'em up wi' a round turn,' s' I; 'He
knows how to deal wi' unreasonable and
wicked men.' I said them very words."

"Saint Paul said 'em before you, Sister Jane,
but you said 'em right, — you said 'em right,"
exclaimed Squire Inchly, heartily.

"Well, I don't set up to judge nobody, but I
don't need no spyglass for to see what's right
in front of my face," said Miss Jane.

Thus these two old people sat and talked about the affairs of their friends and neighbors, — affairs in which they might be said to have almost a personal interest. The conversation turned to other matters; but across the way they saw enacted some of the preliminaries and accompaniments of a mysterious complication that finally became as distressing and as disastrous as a tragedy.

Old Billy Carew continued to gesticulate with his cane and to talk to himself. He desired no other audience. One moment he would be convulsed with laughter; then he would draw himself up proudly, wave his hand imperiously, and seem to be laying down a proposition that demanded great deliberation of thought and accuracy of expression. After awhile his son, apparently growing tired of the humiliating spectacle, left his father to himself, and went over to Squire Inchly's.

Jack Carew was a great favorite with the Squire and his sister. Miss Jane had petted him as a boy; indeed, after the death of his own mother, she had maintained towards him the relations of a foster - mother. His instinct had told him, even when a child, that the asperity of Miss Inchly was merely the humorous mask of a gentle and sensitive heart.

As he flung himself wearily in the chair which Miss Jane had been quick to provide, he seemed, notwithstanding his dejection, to be a very handsome specimen of manhood. His hair was dark, his eyes large and lustrous, his nose straight and firm, and his chin square and energetic. His face was smooth-shaven, and but for the glow of health in his cheeks, his complexion would have been sallow.

"Father has gone to the legislature again," he said with a faint apologetic smile and a motion of the hand toward the scene of the poor old man's alcoholic eloquence.

"Well," said Miss Jane, soothingly, "he hain't the first poor creetur that's flung his welfare to the winds. The Old Boy's mighty busy in these days, but the Almighty hain't dead yit, I reckon, and he'll come along the-reckly and set things to rights."

The young man's face grew gloomy as he looked across the way at his homestead. The house was showing signs of neglect, and the fences were falling away here and there. The jagged splinters of a tall oak whose top had been wrenched off by a storm were outlined against the sky, and an old man babbled and dribbled near by. On the hither side the Cherokee roses bloomed and the birds sang. It seemed as if some horrible nightmare had thrust itself between Jack Carew and the sweet dreams of his youth.

"I trust you are right, Miss Jane," said Jack, after a long pause; "but He will have to come soon if He sets my affairs to rights."

"Don't git down-hearted, Jack," exclaimed Miss Jane, laying her hand upon the young man's arm with a motherly touch. "Them that's big-hearted and broad-shouldered hain't got much to be afear'd of in this world. Have you forgot Rose Gaither, Jack?"

" I have n't forgotten Bradley Gaither," said Jack, frowning darkly, " and I won't forget him in a day, you may depend. Bradley Gaither is at the bottom of all the misery you see there." The young man made a gesture that included the whole horizon.

" Ah, Jack ! " exclaimed Miss Jane, solemnly, " I won't deny but what old Bradley Gaither is been mighty busy runnin' arter the rudiments of the world, but the time was when you 'd kindle up at the bare mention of Rose Gaither's name."

" Shall I tell you the truth, Miss Jane ? " asked Jack Carew, turning to Miss Inchly with a frank, but bashful smile.

" You 've never failed to do that, Jack, when the pinch come."

" Well, this is the pinch, then. But for Rose Gaither I should have sold out here when I first found how matters stood. I could easily sell out now — to Bradley Gaither."

" That 's so, Jack, you could," said Squire Inchly, who had been a sympathetic listener.

"Yes, sir, you could; there ain't no two ways about that."

"But I wouldn't and I won't," continued Jack. "Everybody around here knows my troubles, and I propose to stay here. I haven't forgotten Rose Gaither, Miss Jane, but I'm afraid she has forgotten me. She has changed greatly."

"You look in the glass," said Miss Jane, with a knowing toss of the head, "and you'll see where the change is. Rose was here t' other day, and she stood right in that room there, behind them identical curtains. I wish — but I sha'n't tell the poor child's secrets. I'll say this: the next time you see Rose Gaither a-passin' by, you raise your hat and tell her howdy, and you'll git the sweetest smile that ever man got."

"Miss Jane!" exclaimed Jack Carew, "you are the best woman in the world."

"Except one, I reckon," said Miss Jane, dryly.

Jack Carew rose from his chair, and straight-

ened himself to his full height. He was a new
man. Youth and hope rekindled their fires
in his eyes. The flush of enthusiasm revisited
his face.

" I feel like a new man; I *am* a new man!"
he exclaimed. Then he glanced at the pitiful
figure, maundering and sputtering across the
way. " I am going home," he went on, " and
put father to bed and nurse him and take care
of him just as if — well, just as if I was his
mother."

" The Lord 'll love you for it, Jack," said
Miss Jane, " and so 'll Rose Gaither. When
ever'thing else happens," she continued solemnly, " put your trust in the Lord, and don't
have no misdoubts of Rose."

The superstition that recognizes omens and
portents we are apt to laugh at as vulgar, but it
has an enduring basis in the fact that no circumstance can be regarded as absolutely trivial.
Events apparently the most trifling lead to
the most tremendous results. The wisest of
us know not by what process the casual is

transformed into the dreadful, nor how accident is twisted into fate.

Jack Carew visited the Inchlys almost daily; yet if he had postponed the visit, the purport of which has been given above, the probability is that he would have been spared much suffering; on the other hand, he would have missed much happiness that came to him at a time of life when he was best prepared to appreciate it. He had determined in his own mind to sell the little land and the few negroes he had saved from the wreck his father's extravagance had made; he had determined to sell these, and slip away with his father to a new life in the West; but his conversation with Miss Jane gave him new hope and courage, so that when Bradley Gaither, a few weeks afterwards, offered to buy the Carew place for two or three times its value, he received a curt and contemptuous message of refusal.

Young Carew was high-strung and sensitive even as a boy, and events had only served to develop these traits. When he was compelled to leave college to take charge of his father's affairs, he felt that his name was disgraced forever. He found, however, that all who had known him were anxious to hold up his hands, and to give him such support as one friend is prepared to give another. If the Pinetuckians were simple-minded, they were also sympathetic. There was something gracious as well as wholesome in their attitude. The men somehow succeeded in impressing him with a vague idea that they had passed through just such troubles in their young days. The idea was encouraging, and Jack Carew made the most of it.

But he never thought of Rose Gaither without a sense of deepest humiliation. He had loved Rose when they were school-children together, but his passion had now reached such proportions that he deeply resented the fact that his school-boy love had been so careless and shallow a feeling. Now that circumstances had placed her beyond his reach, he regretted that his youthful love experience was not

17

worthier of the place it held in his remembrance. He could forget that Rose Gaither was the daughter of the man to whom he attributed his troubles, but he could never forget that he himself was the son of a man whose weakness had found him out at an age when manhood ought to have made him strong.

Still, Jack Carew made the most of a bad situation. He had the courage, the endurance, and the hopefulness of youth. He faced his perplexities with at least the appearance of good humor; and if he had his moments of despair, when the skeleton in the jug in the closet paraded in public, Pinetucky never suspected it. The truth is, while Pinetucky was sympathetic and neighborly, it was not inclined to make a great fuss over those who took a dram too much now and then. Intemperance was an evil, to be sure; but even intemperance had its humorous side in those days, and Pinetucky was apt to look at the humorous side.

One fine morning, however, Pinetucky awoke to the fact that it was the centre and scene of

a decided sensation. Rumor pulled on her bonnet and boots, and went gadding about like mad.
Pinetucky was astonished, then perplexed, then
distressed, and finally indignant, as became a
conservative and moral community. A little
after sunrise, Bradley Gaither had galloped up
to Squire Inchly's door with the information
that two bales of cotton had been stolen from
his place the night before.

The facts, as set forth by Bradley Gaither,
were that he had twelve bales of cotton ready
for market. The twelve bales had been loaded
upon three wagons, and the wagons were to
start for Augusta at daybreak. At the last
moment, when everything was ready, the teams
harnessed and the drivers in their seats, it was
discovered that two bales of the cotton were
missing. Fortunately, it had rained during the
night, and Bradley Gaither had waited until it
was light enough to make an investigation. He
found that a wagon had been driven to his
packing-screw. He saw, moreover, that but
one wagon had passed along the road after the

rain, and it was an easy matter to follow the tracks.

The fact of the theft had surprised Squire Inchly, but the details created consternation in his mind. The tracks of the wagon led to the Carew place! Squire Inchly was prompt with a rebuke.

"Why, you've woke up wi' a joke in your mouth, Mr. Gaither. Now that you've spit it out, let's start fresh. A spiteful joke before breakfus' 'll make your flesh crawl arter supper, Mr. Gaither."

Squire Inchly spoke seriously, as became a magistrate. Bradley Gaither's thin lips grew thinner as he smiled.

"I'm as serious as the thieves that stole my cotton, Squire Inchly," he said.

"Two whole bales of cotton in these days is a heavy loss," said the Squire, reflectively. "I hope you'll ketch the inconsiderate parties to the larceny."

"If you will go with me, Squire, we'll call by for Brother Gossett and Colonel Hightower, and if I'm not mistaken we'll find the cotton not far from here."

"Well, sir," said the Squire, indignantly, "you won't find it on the Carew place. I'll go wi' you and welcome. We don't need no search-warrant."

The long and the short of it was that the cotton was found concealed in Jack Carew's rickety barn under a pile of fodder. Of those who joined Bradley Gaither in the search, not one believed that the cotton would be found on the Carew place; and some of them had even gone so far as to suggest to Mr. Gaither that his suspicions had been fathered by his prejudices; but that injured individual merely smiled his cold little smile, and declared that there could be no harm in following the wagon tracks. This was reasonable enough; and the result was that not only was the cotton found, but the wagon standing under the shelter and two mules at the trough in the lot, showed signs of having been lately used.

These things so shocked those who had gone

with Bradley Gaither that they had little to say. They stood confounded. They could not successfully dispute the evidence of their eyes.

They were simple-minded men, and therefore sympathetic. Each one felt ashamed. They did not look into each other's eyes and give utterance to expressions of astonishment. They said nothing; but each one, with the exception of Bradley Gaither, fell into a state of mental confusion akin to awe. When Bradley Gaither, with an air of triumph, asked them if they were satisfied, they said nothing, but turned and walked away one after the other.

They turned and walked away and went to their homes; and somehow, after that, though the sun shone as brightly and the birds fluttered and sang as joyously, a silence fell upon Pinetucky, — a silence full of austerity. The men talked in subdued tones when they met, as though they expected Justice to discharge one of her thunderbolts at their feet; and the women went about their duties with a degree of nervousness that was aptly described by Miss

Jane Inchly long afterwards, when reciting the experiences of that most memorable day in the history of Pinetucky. "I let a sifter drop out 'n my hand," said she, "and I declare to gracious if it did n't sound like a cannon had went off."

In all that neighborhood the Carews, father and son, had but one accuser, and not one apologist. Pinetucky existed in a primitive period, as we are in the habit of believing now, and its people were simple-minded people. In this age of progress and culture morality and justice are arrayed in many refinements of speech and thought. They have been re-adjusted, so to speak, by science; but in Pinetucky in the forties, morality and justice were as robust and as severe as they are in the Bible.

It was not until after the machinery of justice had been set in motion that Pinetucky allowed itself to comment on the case; but the comment was justified by the peculiar conduct of the Carews. When they were confronted

with the facts, — the cotton concealed in the
barn and the warrant in the hands of the sheriff, — old Billy Carew fell a-trembling as though
he had the palsy. Jack had turned pale as
death, and had made a movement toward
Bradley Gaither as though to offer violence;
but when he saw his father shaking so, the
color returned to his face, and he exclaimed
quickly, —

"The warrant is for me alone, Mr. Sheriff.
Pay no attention to father. He is old, and his
mind is weak."

"He's a liar!" the old man screamed, when
he found his voice. "He's a miserable liar!
He never stole that cotton. Don't tetch him!
don't you dast to tetch him! He'll lie to you,
but he won't steal your cotton! Put my name
in that warrant. Bradley Gaither stole my
money and land; I reckon I've got the rights
to steal his cotton."

"He's drunk again," said Jack. "We'll
carry him in the house, and then I'll be ready
to go with you."

But the old man was not carried to the house without a scene. He raved, and screamed, and swore, and finally fell to the ground in a fit of impotent rage, protesting to the last that Jack was a liar. When those who were present had been worked up to the highest pitch of excitement, Bradley Gaither spoke.

"Don't criminate yourself, Jack. I am willing to drop this matter." He appeared to be greatly agitated.

"Drop what matter?" exclaimed young Carew in a passion. "I have a matter with you, sir, that won't be dropped."

"Go your ways, then," said Bradley Gaither; "I've done my duty." With that he mounted his horse, and Jack Carew was left in the hands of the sheriff.

The machinery of the law was not as difficult to set in motion in those days as it is now. There was no delay. Pinetucky was greatly interested in the trial, and during the two days of its continuance delegations of Pinetuckians were present as spectators. Some of these were summoned to testify to the good character of young Carew, and this they did with a simplicity that was impressive; but neither their testimony nor the efforts of the distinguished counsel for the defence, Colonel Peyton Poindexter, had any effect. The facts and the tacit admissions of Jack were against him. Colonel Poindexter's closing speech was long remembered and indeed is alluded to even now, as the most eloquent and impressive ever delivered in the court-house in Rockville; but it failed to convince the jury. A verdict in accordance with the facts and testimony was brought in, and Jack Carew was sentenced to serve a term in the penitentiary at Milledgeville.

The first to bring this information to Pinetucky was Bradley Gaither himself. He stopped at Squire Inchly's for his daughter, and went in.

" What's the news ? " asked Miss Jane.

" Bad, very bad news," said Bradley Gaither.

" Jack ain't hung, I reckon," said Miss Jane.
" My mind tells me, day and night, that the poor boy is innocent as the child that's unborn."

"Innocent or guilty," said Bradley Gaither, "he has been sent to the penitentiary."

Miss Jane gave a quick glance at Rose, and was just in time to catch her as she fell from her chair.

"Ah, poor child!" cried Miss Jane, "her heart is broke!"

"Rose!—Daughter!—Darling!" exclaimed Bradley Gaither, dropping on his knees beside her. "Oh, what is this? What have I done? Speak to her, Miss Inchly! What shall I do?" He was pale as death, and his features worked convulsively.

"Do nothin', Mr. Gaither. You've done more 'n you can undo a'ready. You've took and give that poor boy over for to be persecuted, Mr. Gaither, and now the innocent suffers and the wicked goes scotch-free."

Bradley Gaither covered his face with his hands and groaned aloud.

"What have I done? What have I done?" he cried.

Miss Jane supported the girl in her strong

arms with a grim display of affection, but her attitude towards Bradley Gaither was uncompromising.

"Don't alarm yourself, Mr. Gaither," she said; "this poor child 'll come round quick enough. Folks don't fling off their misery this easy!"

Rose revived after awhile, but she seemed to have no desire to talk to her father. After a copious use of camphor, Miss Jane fixed the girl comfortably on the lounge, and she lay there and gazed at the ceiling, the picture of wide-eyed despair. Bradley Gaither paced the floor like one distracted. His sighs were heart-rending. When Miss Jane succeeded in getting him out of the room, he paced up and down the entry, moving his lips and groaning as though in great mental agony. Failing to understand what emotions he was at the mercy of, Miss Jane failed to sympathize with him. To her mind, his display of grief bore no sort of proportion to the cause, and she had a woman's contempt for any manifestation of weakness in man, even the weakness of grief.

"I'll pray to the Lord to forgive me!" he cried out piteously.

"That's right," exclaimed Miss Jane, in her decisive way. "But if the grace of pra'r was in the hinges of the knee, I know a heap of folks that'd be mighty easy in the mind."

Every word she spoke cut like a knife, but not until long after did Miss Inchly realize the fact. When she did realize it, it is to be feared she hugged the remembrance of it to her bosom with a sort of grim thankfulness that Providence had so happily fashioned her words and directed her tongue.

As time passed on, the Pinetuckians became aware that a great change had come over both Bradley Gaither and his daughter. The father grew old before his time, and fell into a decline, as his neighbors expressed it. The daughter grew more beautiful, but it was beauty of a kind that belongs to devoutness; so that, in contemplating it, the minds of men were led in the direction of mercy and charity and all manner of good deeds.

One night, a year or more after the trial and sentence of Jack Carew, a negro on horseback rode to Squire Inchly's door, and said that his master, Bradley Gaither, desired the Squire to come to him at once. The worthy magistrate was prompt to obey the summons; and when he arrived at the Gaither place, he found that the preacher and other neighbors had also been summoned. Bradley Gaither lay upon his bed, surrounded by these, and it was plain to see that his sands of life had nearly run out. He presented a spectacle of dissolution calculated to arouse the sympathies of those who stood around his bed.

After Squire Inchly arrived, Bradley Gaither lay a little while with his eyes closed as in a dream. Then he motioned to his daughter, who drew from beneath his pillow a few sheets of letter-paper stained and blotted with ink. These she handed to the minister.

" Read it aloud," said Bradley Gaither. The

minister, with some degree of embarrassment, adjusted his spectacles and read : —

"With this paper will be found my last will and testament. I am unhappy, but I should be less miserable if I knew I could put such meaning in these lines as no man could misunderstand. I have sinned against an innocent man, I have sinned against my dear daughter, I have sinned against myself, I have sinned against God. I have been guilty of a great wrong, and though I cannot forgive myself, yet I hope to be forgiven. John Carew, who is now in prison, is an innocent man. I coveted his land. In my worldly-mindedness, I set my heart upon his possessions. I offered him double their value. I thought he treated me with contempt, and then I hit upon a plan to drive him out. I carried the cotton to his barn and hid it. He knew no more about it than any honest man. But, as God is my judge, I did not foresee the end. I thought he would compromise and sell the land and go away. At the last the law took the matter out of my hands. John Carew believes that he is suffering punishment in place of his father; but William Carew is as honest as his son, and no man could be honester than that. I, Bradley Gaither, being in my right mind and of sound memory, do hereby charge myself with the crime for which John Carew has been adjudged guilty. Let the disgrace of it be attached to me alone. The sin of it I hope a merciful God will forgive."

This document was duly signed and witnessed. When the preacher reached the end, he said, " Let us pray ; " and while that prayer, as fervent as simplicity could make it, was ascending heavenward, the soul of Bradley Gaither took its flight.

" I glanced at him arter the breath left him," said Squire Inchly, relating the facts to his sister, " and he looked like a man that had shook hisself free from a heap of worriment. I hope he 's at peace, I do, from the bottom of my heart."

The confession was received with great won-

der in Pinetucky; but there was not one among
the Pinetuckians who did not believe that Bradley Gaither was a better man at bottom than
his life had shown him to be, — not one, indeed, who did not believe that his grievous
errors were among the dispensations which an
all-wise Providence employs to chasten the
proud and humble the vainglorious.

When Jack Carew returned to his friends,
he made his way straight to Squire Inchly's.
He was not much changed, but the sight of
him gave Miss Jane the cue for tears. These,
however, she dried immediately, and, with a
smile that Jack remembered long, motioned
towards the little sitting-room.

"Go in there, Jack. A man ought n't to
grumble at waitin' for his dinner if he knows
he'll git pie."

In the little sitting-room Rose Gaither was
waiting for him.